THE BEAR'S BRAVE OMEGA

A.J. CANE

ONE

MILO

I'd made a terrible mistake. I never should have agreed to this date.

As he droned on about his love of shooting small fluffy animals, I glanced around to see if I could find a quick way to escape. Unfortunately, no opportunity presented itself. We were seated at a picnic table outside a barbecue place on the edge of the woods. He'd been the one to drive us here, which meant I was reliant on him for a ride home.

I wished—not for the first time—that I'd stayed in today. No matter how lonely I was, dating random guys off apps wasn't the answer. This would be the first and only time I made that mistake. My date, Tomas, had looked all right on paper, but in the flesh, he gave me the creeps. Not to mention the fact he was boastful, abrasive, and enjoyed the sound of his own voice.

"Did I tell you about the time I shot a wild stag and had to carry it for two days to get it home?" he asked, leaning toward me across the table.

"No," I murmured, afraid to mention how unhygienic I thought it was to keep a dead animal with him for so long without any means of refrigeration. How had he been able to sleep with the poor thing's corpse beside him?

"It was June. Maybe three years ago. Or four. I can't remember for sure."

I glanced down and rolled my eyes. I didn't care how many years ago it was. Why should I, when he'd already made it clear he didn't care about the details of my life? He hadn't asked me a single thing about myself since he'd picked me up. When I'd decided to open up and share my real thoughts about hunting—that I didn't think I'd be able to do it because I couldn't kill anything—he'd laughed in my face. Then he'd patted my hand and said that if I was a good omega and let my alpha provide for me, I wouldn't ever have to hunt.

I'd bitten back a retort, knowing it wouldn't go down well. I may be an omega, but I'd been taking care of myself since I was young and doing a damn sight better at it than anyone else had so far.

Suddenly, Tomas stood. He rounded the table and slid onto the bench beside me. He reached across to drag his plate over, leaned close to me, and sniffed.

"Damn, you smell good."

A shiver crawled up my spine. What kind of person sniffed someone they'd just met? I shuffled along the bench, trying to put space between us. I may smell good, but Tomas definitely didn't. He had a strong odor that I couldn't quite place. Something like wet fur and dirt. Maybe he had a dog. Or maybe he'd been in the woods slaughtering animals before he'd picked me up. That sounded on-brand.

If only I'd thought to bring my own car. I doubted there were many taxis out here in the middle of nowhere.

"I feel a connection between us," Tomas said, erasing the space I'd managed to build. He tried to hold my gaze.

There was something scary about his eyes. They were too green, with a tinge of yellow. Perhaps he was wearing contacts. "I think you're meant for me, omega."

I tried to stand. "I'm afraid I don't..."

He caged me in with his arms. I stared at him in disbelief as a pair of fangs protruded between his lips. I blinked, but they were still there.

What the hell?

Were they real, or some kind of sick prank? Whatever the case, I wasn't about to hang around and find out.

"Fuck." I tried to back away from him, but he'd trapped me in place. I looked around for something I could use to defend myself. Why had I let him bring me out back when all the other patrons were inside?

There were no knives on the table, but there was an open bottle of hot sauce. Perhaps I could hit him with it.

He leaned closer and bared those fangs. They were real. Holy fuck.

I screamed. What the hell was he?

He lunged toward me, his fangs aimed at my neck, but I grabbed the open bottle of hot sauce and tossed it in his face. His teeth scraped my skin and retreated as the hot sauce coated his nose and eyes. He shrieked, the sound almost inhuman, and clutched at his face. I yanked myself away and bolted into the woods, desperation clawing at my gut. I had to escape him. Somehow, I knew that if I didn't, I'd regret it for the rest of my life.

I stumbled through the undergrowth, sticks tearing at my skin, struggling to keep my footing on the uneven ground. I could hear Tomas behind me, swearing, but I couldn't tell if he was coming after me. Fuck, why had I come this way instead of running into the barbecue joint where there would have been people to help?

The ground disappeared beneath me and I stumbled

down an embankment, knocking my knee on a rock before splashing into a frigid stream. I gasped as icy water engulfed my body, instantly soaking my jeans and shirt and covering my face. I burst through the surface, spluttering, and hauled a breath into my lungs.

Shit.

This wasn't good. I'd seen nature documentaries. I knew about hypothermia. It could set in quickly when someone was wet and exposed, especially in a place like this. I should turn around and go back. Try to find someone who could help. But what if I ran into Tomas again?

Those crazy teeth flashed through my mind and my stomach sank. If there were any chance that hadn't been a figment of my overactive imagination then I couldn't risk running into him again. He might have been about to tear my throat out. Even if they were some kind of weird implant, they could hurt me.

Wasn't this just my goddamned luck?

I gritted my teeth. Time to prioritize. Priority one. Avoid Tomas. But how? I thought quickly. I'd heard that following streams and rivers made it more difficult for people to track you. Tomas was a hunter, so presumably he'd know a bit about tracking. I was sure I'd left an obvious trail as I'd blundered through the bush, but perhaps this stream was a blessing in disguise. If I kept moving and found somewhere I could get dry, I might be safe.

I glanced at the embankment I'd fallen down, wondering how close behind Tomas was—if he was following me at all. I debated whether to remove my jeans. Was it safer if I kept them on as a barrier from the elements, or if I removed them because they were waterlogged and freezing?

Keep them on, I decided.

I made my way to the edge of the steam and walked in

the water. My toes were already going numb, but if this was my best shot at living to see another sunrise then I wasn't going to wuss out. I stumbled and stepped on something sharp. I swore, but I couldn't see any blood, so I put my foot back down and continued walking.

One step at a time.

One step at a time.

One step at a time.

I repeated it over and over in my head. I could do this. I'd be okay. I'd survived everything else life had thrown at me, so conquering the world's worst date would be nothing but a blip on the radar. One day I'd laugh about this.

Maybe.

On the other hand, I might die out here. Alone. The same way I'd lived. My face curled into a snarl. I'd made one attempt to connect with someone and this had happened. Perhaps I should accept the message the universe kept sending me. I was supposed to be on my own.

CHAPTER

TWO

EVERETT

I shook my head in disgust as my team and I—the Grizzly Ridge Search and Rescue squad—left our liaison officer speaking to the wolf shifter who'd called us in and headed toward the edge of the woods.

"Something isn't right with that one," I muttered to my brother Garrick. "He's a wolf. Surely he should be able to track his mate and bring him home safely without us interfering."

Garrick shrugged. "Maybe he wants to respect his mate's space. He did say they argued and that the guy wasn't happy when he headed into the woods."

I scoffed. "No shifter respect's their mate's space if they're genuinely worried about them. It's not in our DNA."

"So maybe it's not that," Garrick allowed. "Maybe he's a city wolf and isn't used to using his nose."

I side-eyed him. "Does he look like a city wolf to you?"

"Nah." He sighed. "But so what? Maybe he's lazy, or maybe he was cursed by a warlock and doesn't have a properly developed sense of smell."

I rolled my shoulders. "I don't like it."

6

He grinned and jostled me. "You don't like anything, Ev." He stopped walking and turned to face me. "Here's how I see it. Whether the wolf is telling us the truth or not, we can't leave a human omega alone in the woods at night. We need to find him. Once we do, he can clear up any misunderstandings."

I nodded in acknowledgment. He had a point. Humans were vulnerable. Especially omegas, who weren't as strong as alphas and smelled like prey.

Garrick gestured the others to us and spoke loudly, assigning roles to each of us and explaining where he wanted us to prioritize our search. He'd already shown us the wolf's car, where we'd been able to sniff hints of the human omega's scent, although much of it had been masked by the strong odor of wolf. Apparently the wolf, Tomas, didn't have any of his mate's personal items which we could use to get a clearer scent—another thing that made me suspicious.

When Garrick finished, we all stripped out of our clothes and placed them in a plastic box that would remain here for when we returned, then we shifted. I felt the familiar disconcerting sense of being too much beast confined within a too-small figure for a few seconds, and then my bear took over. My limbs thickened and sprouted fur. My head rose farther from the ground and my vision improved until I could see nearly as well as if it were daylight. I lowered myself to all fours and loped into the woods, following the directions Garrick had given me. As the squad's best tracker, I would take point.

It was easy to find where the omega had crashed through the bush. Twigs were snapped, leaves disturbed, and footsteps left in the dirt. It didn't seem as if he'd walked off as the wolf had said. More like he'd bolted into the woods without looking or caring where he was going. I paused to register his scent. It was sweet, with hints of cherry. I inhaled deeply. Gods, he smelled good.

Get it together.

I followed his path until he reached an embankment, where it looked like he may have fallen. My gut twisted with concern, confusing me. I wasn't usually someone who let my feelings get in the way, but I hated the thought of the omega who smelled of cherries being in pain.

I eased down the embankment and found a spot where his scent was concentrated, as if he'd lain there for a moment. I pressed my nose against it and breathed it in greedily.

Mate, my bear whispered.

I shook my head. It couldn't be.

Mate.

I reminded my bear that the omega already had a mate —the wolf—but my bear didn't like that. I was seized by a burning need to find the omega. Find him, ensure his safety, and then destroy his false mate.

Mine. My mate. Ours.

Okay, okay, I got it. The human wasn't the wolf's mate. He was ours. Which meant that the wolf had lied. But first it meant I had to find my mate before he got hypothermia or fell down another embankment with a more lethal result.

I followed my mate's scent to the stream and crossed over, but there was no trace of sweetness and cherries on the other bank. I glanced back at the stream. He must have walked along it. Had he realized it would obscure his scent? Or had he just hoped it would lead him somewhere he could find help? Either way, my mate was smart.

Ours.

My bear chuffed in pleasure.

Later, I told it. *First, I have to find him.*

I navigated the stream for an hour, until it passed by a rocky outcropping. I caught a hint of cherries carried on the wind and I splashed out of the water, barreling toward the rocks. My mate's scent grew stronger with every step. I paced the edge of the outcropping until I spotted a small figure huddled in a crevice in one of the largest rocks. My heart skipped.

Our mate.

The omega had pale blue eyes, the shade of glacier melt, and dark brown hair that was plastered to his scalp. It was difficult to determine his build, but based on the way he'd wedged himself into the rocks, he must be petite. He hugged his jean-clad legs closer to his chest as I approached, trying to retreat further into the crevice.

"Nice bear," he said softly. "Good bear. You don't have to eat me."

I cocked my head, confused, but realized he must not be able to tell I was a shifter rather than one of the normal grizzlies that roamed the area.

His teeth chattered and a shudder tore through his body. "I wouldn't make a good meal."

Protect.

For once, my bear and I were in total agreement. Our mate needed us to warm him and get him back to safety, but first, I needed to alert my team that I'd found him. I trotted away, hoping I wouldn't scare him so much if I put more space between us. I reared back and roared as loud as I could—our signal that I'd located the missing person. Several distant roars came back to me, so I knew my team-mates would be on their way soon. I turned and moved slowly toward the beautiful human, keeping my head low so he wouldn't perceive me as a threat.

As I came within touching distance, I tried to nuzzle him. I needed him to let me get close if I was going to warm him. But those pretty blue eyes rolled back in his head and he slumped against the rock in a dead faint.

Damn.

I maneuvered him out of the tight space and curled around his body. As I'd assumed, he was ice-cold. But even in this condition, he was the best thing I'd ever smelled.

Claim.

Not yet. My beast wanted nothing more than to sink his teeth into the human and make him ours, but the other side of me knew I couldn't do that. If he chose us, I wanted him to do it willingly, not because I got carried away by my instincts and took advantage of the situation.

A shiver racked him, and I cuddled closer. I expected him to open his eyes at any minute, but he didn't. The lack of response worried me. I was tempted to carry him out myself, but that wasn't how the team operated. I had to stay put until the others arrived.

When they did, Francis was the first to appear. He was younger than the rest of us and moved faster. He loped toward me, his gaze fastened on the omega.

I growled.

Francis stopped and looked at me questioningly.

I growled again and shifted the omega closer. I didn't seem able to stop.

"Everett," Garrick barked, and I glanced over to see he'd arrived and had already shifted into his human form. "Let us help the boy."

I growled again, unable to help myself, but hung my head to show Garrick I didn't mean to challenge him. Knowing I needed to shift so I could explain, I slunk away from the omega. Immediately, Francis moved to replace me. I lunged forward, but another bear blocked me. I shifted.

"Sorry," I panted, my hands on my thighs. "He's my mate. My bear wants to protect him."

Garrick's eyebrows rose. "Your mate?" He glanced at the human, who Francis was hovering beside tentatively. "Are you sure?"

"Yes."

"Then that wolf's got a lot of explaining to do."

CHAPTER

THREE

MILO

I woke slowly, becoming conscious of warm blankets cocooned around me and a pillow so soft it felt like a cloud. I smiled, my eyes still closed, and started a languid morning stretch, only to stop as pain flashed through me. I opened my eyes and blinked as they adjusted to the light. A bedroom came into focus, with cream-colored walls, light-gray carpet, and a powder-blue bedspread. I'd never seen this room before.

I had no idea where I was.

I tried to move again and everything twinged. My entire body seemed to ache from the inside out, and my skin was sensitive, each brush of the fabric causing discomfort. I raised my arm and winced. Dozens of scratches created a latticework across the skin, some shallow and superficial, others deeper. What had happened? I tried to remember, but my head throbbed. I recalled my awful date. His posturing and rudeness. Another image flickered through my mind. Had he tried to bite me? I could have sworn I'd seen fangs between his lips.

12

"Can't be," I whispered, the words barely a rasp because my throat was dry.

I must have imagined the teeth. Perhaps I'd had a nervous breakdown. I shut my eyes and tried to concentrate on what had happened next. I'd fled into the woods—that must have been where the scratches had come from, although I'd been running on adrenaline at the time and hadn't noticed.

I'd fallen. There had been a stream, and then a hollow in a rock. What else?

A bear.

My eyes flew open again. A big grizzly bear had cornered me, and after that, everything went black. How had I gotten here?

The bedroom door eased inward and a matronly woman with a kind face and faded brown hair swept into the room, carrying a tray.

"Oh, good, you're awake," she said upon seeing me.

I tried to sit up.

"Don't move." She made a tsking sound and placed the tray on a cupboard beneath the window, then came over and helped ease me into a seated position. "Lean forward."

I did as she said and she plumped the cushions behind my back. When I relaxed against them, several of my muscles twinged. I'd probably used muscles that had never seen action before while I'd been running through the woods. Fitness had never been one of my strengths. The fall wouldn't have helped either.

"Where am I?" I asked.

"Shh."

She passed me a glass of water, hovering close by as though she thought I'd drop it. I drank greedily, emptying it, and she took it back from me.

"Is that better?" she asked.

"Yes, thank you."

"Good." She sat on the edge of the bed and angled herself to face me. "I'm Melinda. You're in my home. I must say, it's a pleasure to see you awake. You had us worried for a while there."

"Us?" I wrung my hands, not liking the fact I still didn't know where I was or why, regardless of how pleasant Melinda seemed.

"Two of my sons were on the search and rescue team that found you," she explained. "You were passed out and borderline hypothermic. They brought you back here to recover and the local doctor came to check on you. He said you just need time to rest and recover, but other than that, you ought to be fine."

I nodded. That was good to know, but I hadn't really felt as though any serious harm had been done. I was just sore, and potentially delusional. "Thank you. I appreciate you taking care of me. If there's anything I can do to repay you—"

"Don't be ridiculous." Melinda scowled as if I'd insulted her. "You can repay us by taking it easy and not pushing yourself too hard."

I pursed my lips. That would be difficult considering I needed to get back to the city so I could work on Monday. Assuming it wasn't Monday already. "What day is it?"

"Sunday." Her expression softened. "We're in Grizzly Ridge. Do you know where that is?"

"No, ma'am." I shook my head. "But I thought I saw a grizzly yesterday, so that makes sense."

Her eyes widened. "Of course you did. The—"

A man strode in, cutting her off before she finished speaking. He was massive, with a presence that seemed to suck up all the space in the room. I stared at him. He drew my gaze like an open flame. He was the sexiest man I'd ever seen, but not in a cookie-cutter way. His eyes were an intense brown and were locked on me like nothing else existed. His dark hair was a shaggy mess, and a beard concealed his jawline, but where Tomas had been dirty and unkempt, this alpha was gorgeously masculine.

"You're awake." His nostrils flared as he spoke, and his voice rumbled through me, low and delicious. "Thank Gods."

He stalked toward me. The way he moved reminded me of a predator, but I wasn't afraid of him. For some reason, his presence made me feel safer than I ever had before. I wanted to beg him to crawl into the bed and hold me, but that was crazy. I couldn't invite a rugged stranger into my bed. Going out with a stranger was what had gotten me into this situation in the first place.

"How do you feel?" the man asked.

Melinda shuffled aside and let him take her place. One of his hands twitched, as though he wanted to reach for me, but he shoved it into the pocket of his jacket instead.

"Everything hurts," I told him, compelled to be honest for reasons I didn't understand. "And I'm hungry."

"Momma brought you breakfast," he said, nodding toward the tray. "It's oatmeal, to rebuild your strength."

Melinda got the tray and set it on Milo's lap. "Eat up. There's more if you need it. You don't have any allergies, do you?"

"No, ma'am. No allergies."

She laughed. "You don't have to 'ma'am' me. Just call me Melinda or Momma Melinda. All my boys do."

"Okay." I glanced at the man, wondering if he was one of "her boys." I'd hardly consider him to be a boy. "I'm Milo."

"Milo." He repeated my name fervently, like a prayer. "I'm Everett. Momma's favorite son."

Melinda rolled her eyes. "So you'd like to think." She smiled at me. "Everett is the one who found you yesterday. He brought you back."

This big, sexy beast had carried me out of the woods and I'd been unconscious for the whole time? Damn.

"Thank you."

"You're welcome, Milo." His hand twitched again and he closed his eyes for a moment and tilted his head. Through the collar of his jacket, I caught a glimpse of a tattoo. "I'm just grateful we found you in time. It gets cold out there at night."

"I am, too." I hated to think what might have happened otherwise. I was just surprised the bear hadn't eaten me. Or perhaps I'd hallucinated him as well as Tomas's fangs.

Everett gazed at me intently. "We didn't release you into your mate's care because his story about how you came to be in the woods didn't add up. We wanted to make sure you were safe."

"My mate?" I asked. "Do you mean like a friend?"

Everett's thick brows drew together. He looked as confused as I felt. "I meant Tomas."

"Oh." I pulled a face. "Him. We were on a first date, and it wasn't going well. Next thing I knew, the guy was trying to bite me." I pictured those fangs and shivered.

"Are you cold?" Everett asked.

"No." I forced a smile. "This bed is perfect, thank you."

"Where did Tomas try to bite you?"

I peeled back the collar of the pajama shirt I now realized wasn't mine. Of course it wasn't. The clothes I'd been wearing must have been soaked. These probably belonged to one of Momma's boys—presumably Everett and his brothers.

"Here." There was a slight graze where the teeth had caught my skin as I pulled away. I heard a quick intake of breath and looked back at Everett. For a second, I could have sworn his eyes were gold, but then I blinked and they were back to normal.

I'm going crazy.

"Did he do that?" Everett touched the mark, surprisingly gentle for such a big man. I wanted to close my eyes and ask him to stroke me all over.

"Yeah." I held still, determined not to shudder and give away how much his touch affected me.

He cleared his throat and withdrew his hand. "So, just to be clear, you're not together and you don't want to see him again?"

"That's right."

"Great." He made a strange noise in the back of his throat, almost like a purr. Weird.

"Anyway, you don't need to worry about me." I opened the lid on the oatmeal and picked up the spoon. "I'll finish this and then I can call a taxi or find a bus and head back home. Thanks so much for your hospitality. You went above and beyond."

Everett's eyes narrowed. "You need to rest. There's no hurry for you to leave. Why don't you eat and then we can talk about what comes next?"

I opened my mouth to answer but he stood abruptly and strode out. I turned to Melinda, hoping for an explanation.

She just shrugged. "Everett isn't much of a talker. He's right, though. You eat up and have a hot shower. You'll feel so much better after." She made her way to the door, then paused. "Do you like coffee? Tea? Hot cocoa?"

"Coffee would be great, but only if it's not a nuisance."

She beamed. "None at all. I'll make it now, and I'll bring it in along with a towel and a washcloth. You can borrow some of my son Danny's clothes. You're a similar size."

The back of my eyes stung and I blinked rapidly. It had been so long since someone had fussed over me like this. It felt really good.

"Thank you, Melinda."

"You're very welcome, Milo."

She left, and I couldn't help wishing she'd stayed a little longer so I could enjoy her mothering.

"Get over it," I muttered to myself. It was a hazard of being a foster kid. If anyone showed me the slightest bit of affection, I wanted to lap it up like a greedy cat. But Melinda wasn't my mom and I was an adult who could take care of himself.

FOUR

EVERETT

I drove the short distance from my parents' place to the precinct that housed both the search and rescue headquarters and the police station. I needed to tell the team what Milo had said about the wolf.

Milo.

My heart thumped, recalling the longing in his eyes as he'd looked at me. My bear had wanted to preen, but there had been a wariness about him too. He seemed like a shy, sweet man, but my instincts told me he'd seen a lot of the world's underbelly while I hadn't been around to protect him. I hated that, but at least I knew he'd be safe from now on. My bear and I would protect him with our life.

I parked out behind the building and let myself in the rear door, heading straight for Garrick's office. I knocked once and he called for me to come in.

"Milo is awake," I told him, hearing the softness in my own voice as it wrapped around my mate's name. *Milo.* It was as sweet as he was.

"How is he?" Garrick asked, placing his pen in a holder and stretching his back. Bear shifters weren't built for office work, but it was a hazard of being the boss that he sometimes had to put aside his preference for the outdoors.

"Achy and on edge." I wished I could take away his pain. Shifters healed quickly from everything except injuries from silver weapons, but humans weren't as lucky. I supposed I'd have a lifetime to get accustomed to seeing my human mate suffer through discomfort that I never had to deal with. A sobering thought.

"Now that he's awake, are you still convinced he's your mate?"

"More than ever." There was just something about him that made me want to cradle him in my arms and never let him go. Well, that, and stuff him full of my cock until he couldn't think of any man other than me. I cleared my throat and willed myself not to get hard while my brother was in the room. Considering he'd be able to smell my arousal, it would be awkward as hell. "He said it was his first date with the wolf."

Garrick raised an eyebrow. "So, they're not mates."

A growl tore from between my lips. "Sorry." I tilted my head to the side submissively so he'd know I meant no harm. My bear loathed the idea of the wolf's dirty paws on our mate. "No, they're not. According to Milo, the wolf tried to bite him and that was why he ran into the woods."

Garrick rose to his feet, a rumble emanating from his chest. "He tried to mate Milo without consent?"

I felt my eyes change, my bear surging to the surface at the thought of how close my Milo had come to being forced into a bond he didn't want. "Yeah, I think so."

"Shit." He glanced at me, and his eyes flashed a shade of gold that matched mine. We were both sensitive about violence toward omegas, especially since our younger brother, Danny, had recently gotten out of an abusive relationship. "We need to track Tomas down and let his pack know so they can deal with him. That's unacceptable behavior."

"Want me to get Zander?" I asked.

He nodded. "Bring him here."

"Got it."

I left Garrick's office and strode down the hall and around the corner, where it merged with the police station, and nearly bowled into Zander coming the other way.

"Hey, man." I steadied him with one hand. "You got a moment? Garrick and I need to see you."

"Sure." He gestured for me to go first. The corridor was narrow, and Zander was even broader than me, so we didn't fit well side by side.

In Garrick's office, we filled Zander in on what we'd learned.

"I'll get Clay to drop by the hotel where Tomas said he was staying and ask him a couple of questions," Zander said, reaching for his radio. "He's in the area."

He spoke to Clay, and we all waited while the deputy stopped at the hotel and went inside. He didn't check in for several minutes, during which I assumed he was speaking to the staff. When he came back, he sounded flustered.

"Sheriff, the wolf isn't here. The manager says no one fitting his description has checked in over the past few days."

"He lied to us." Garrick swore under his breath.

"Thanks, Clay," Zander said into the radio. "Appreciate you checking."

"No problem, sir."

Zander glanced from me to Garrick. "If the wolf lied, it's because he's hiding something. If he tried to mate with Milo once, there's no reason he won't try again. It's possible he's going feral or having some kind of breakdown. We need to keep an eye on Milo and make sure he isn't in danger." He turned back to me. "I'm sure you can manage that."

"Absolutely." No deranged wolf would be getting near my mate. "I'll speak to Dad about it."

Our father was the clan Alpha and all decisions about who came and went from our township had to be run through him.

"Great." He clapped my shoulder. "I'm going to ask around and see if I can find out where the wolf came from. I've heard rumors of a rogue pack in Moonlight Cove, so someone in that area might have useful information."

"A rogue pack?" My bear bristled. Moonlight Cove was only a couple of towns over, and a rogue wolf pack could be dangerous. Rogue packs tended to move from one place to another, eliminating the local shifter groups and using their resources before going somewhere new. We didn't want rogues anywhere near Grizzly Ridge.

"So far they haven't done much damage," Zander said. "At least, not around here."

"You two sound like you've got everything under control," Garrick said. "Let me know if you need anything. Otherwise, I'll trust you to handle it."

Zander and I nodded. While Zander was the largest in our family, Garrick had the most dominant personality. When he spoke, people listened. I suspected he'd be the Alpha one day in the not-too-distant-future, when Dad was ready to step down.

We parted ways and I headed back to my parents' place, parking outside and taking the stairs two at a time in a rush to speak to my father. Now that I could smell Milo's delicious scent again, I wanted nothing more than to go with him, but I needed Dad's approval first.

"Come in," Dad called when I knocked on his door.

I inclined my head. "Alpha."

He waved his hand at the seat opposite him. "Sit."

I did, and briefly summed up what Garrick, Zander, and I had discovered so far.

"Zander is right," Dad said. "Milo needs to remain here until we can be sure he's safe."

I sighed and pinched the bridge of my nose. "How are we supposed to convince him of that when he doesn't know the danger he's in? I'm pretty sure he doesn't know about shifters." The way he'd asked about mates had given him away. Most people familiar with shifters knew about mates.

Dad thought for a moment. "Perhaps you could tell him that this Tomas fellow has a history of violence and the police are looking for him. If you're right, and he doesn't know about us, then we need to keep it that way for now."

"But he's my mate, so he's going to find out eventually." Although Gods only knew how I was supposed to break that news to him. If I just came out and said it, he'd think I was crazy, and if I showed him, there was a good chance he'd be scared. He'd been afraid of my bear when we'd rescued him, and I hadn't liked it.

"Be that as it may, we need to learn more about what type of person he is first."

I shoved my hand into my pocket, resisting the urge to clench it into a fist. He was right. Unfortunately, that meant one more barrier between me and my mate.

Claim, my bear grumbled.

I gritted my teeth. *We have to wait.*

But the beast didn't understand that, and honestly, I just wanted to kiss the hell out of Milo and lock him away from the world. Instead, I'd have to convince him to stay here—in a perfect stranger's house—and figure out how to show him the truth without freaking him out. Why couldn't this mate thing come with a guidebook?

CHAPTER

FIVE

MILO

The hot water stung my cuts and scrapes, but it felt wonderful to wash away the dirt and sweat from the woods. Someone had wiped down my face and arms—presumably whoever had put me to bed—but other than that, I was a mess.

When everything was clean and the scent of lemon lingered in the air from the soap, I turned the water off and toweled dry. Melinda had given me a pair of gray sweatpants and a faded T-shirt to wear. I pulled the pants up and tied the drawstring around the waist because they were slightly too big. I rolled up the hem and carefully eased the shirt over my head. The shirt was a better fit than the pants.

With nothing else for it, I opened the bathroom door and stepped out into the hall. I made my way through the house, drawn by the smell of cookies coming from the kitchen. When I entered, Melinda stood at the kitchen counter, shifting freshly baked chocolate chip cookies from a baking tray to a cooling rack. She slipped a couple onto a small plate and turned toward me, smiling.

"Here, darling." She passed me the plate. "Why don't you sit at the breakfast bar and tell me about yourself."

"Thank you." I seemed to be saying that a lot, but Melinda had been going out of her way to be kind to me and I wasn't used to that. I wouldn't let it pass unnoticed. I sat on a bar stool that was so high my feet dangled in the air, and then touched the edge of a cookie. Too hot to eat. I pushed the plate away a few inches so I wouldn't be tempted and looked up. "I'm not very interesting, really."

"Nonsense." Melinda leaned against the other side of the breakfast bar. Between her plump physique and the fact she smelled of cookies, she reminded me of mothers from books and movies. The type I'd always dreamed of but never had. I bet Melinda's sons had a normal, loving upbringing. Unlike mine. "Why don't we start with where you're from?"

"I live in Grayton." I figured telling her that much wouldn't do any harm.

She pulled a face. "I've never liked the city much myself. Do you prefer it to the country?"

I shrugged. "I've never lived outside of the city, so I don't know."

Her lips curled into a smile. "I bet we could make a country boy out of you."

I didn't know what to make of that, so I stayed silent and touched the cookie again. Still too hot. "Have you guys always lived here?"

"Yes." Her smile turned fond. "My husband Aaron and I both grew up here. We married straight out of high school and started raising our boys." She tilted her head quizzically. "Do your parents live in Grayton too?"

I stiffened. "No, ma'am."

Although they could, to be fair. I had no idea. I didn't

know who they were, or whether they were even alive. All I knew was that they hadn't wanted me. Story of my life.

Footsteps sounded in the hall and another omega hurried into the kitchen. My shoulders relaxed. I was grateful for the interruption. Melinda was probably just trying to be nice, but I didn't like to be asked questions. In my experience, nothing good came of it.

The omega was grinning—enough that it made me wonder what was going on. He swept gorgeous, dark hair away from his face and a dimple appeared in his cheek. He looked like the type of omega I wished I was. Beautiful and undamaged. Envy rolled through me, but I tried to tamp it down. It boiled back to the surface when it occurred to me that this omega might belong to the alpha I'd met earlier. Everett. I didn't like that idea. I knew it was a pipe dream, but for some reason, my heart seemed to have locked onto Everett like a lifeline.

"Good morning, Danny," Melinda said, and most of the envy drained away. This was another of her sons. The one whose clothes I'd been offered.

Danny crossed the space between us in a few steps, his body language giving the impression he was going to hug me, but he stopped just short. "It sounds like you had the date from hell," he said. "Some alphas are awful, right?"

I nodded mutely.

He stuck out his hand. "I'm Danny. It's so nice to meet you. Momma has told me all about you."

"She has?" I shook his hand, dropping it again quickly. He seemed nice, but I wasn't much for human contact... unless it came from a particular, growly alpha. *No, don't think of him.*

Melinda rolled her eyes. "Just that Everett and Garrick had to rescue you from the woods after your date tried to attack you."

"Oh." I bit my lip. "I feel a bit silly, actually. Like maybe I overreacted."

"You absolutely did not." Danny pulled another stool over and sat beside me. "If the guy was giving you bad vibes and tried something you didn't want, you were right to get out of there." He flashed me another dimpled smile. "Just maybe run into town instead of away from it next time."

I flushed. "I'll keep that in mind." Not that there would be a "next time."

I picked up one of the cookies, which had cooled enough to touch, and offered the other to Danny, who beamed with delight and bit into it immediately.

"Danny, those are for my guest," Melinda chastised.

Danny looked unrepentant. "He offered."

"I'm happy to share," I said quickly.

Melinda's expression softened. "You're such a sweetheart." At the other side of the house, a door shut, and Melinda straightened. "No doubt that's Everett."

I tried to school my features but based on Danny's sly smile, he noticed my anticipation. I stared at the counter, my face heating with embarrassment. I wanted to keep my attraction to Everett to myself. He was out of my league on a good day, so considering he'd seen me at my worst, he couldn't possibly be interested in me. I kept my gaze down as footfalls sounded on the tiled floor, suggesting Everett had entered the room.

"Milo?"

That delicious voice rumbled through me and despite my discomfort with being in an unfamiliar setting with people I didn't know, and the aches and pains throughout my body, my cock twitched behind the sweatpants. I prayed that I wouldn't get completely hard because these pants hid nothing.

"Yes?" I raised my eyes cautiously and found that

Everett had replaced Melinda in front of me. He was hunched over so his eyes were nearly level with mine. They burned with that same intensity I'd sensed radiating from him this morning. Self-preservation instincts told me to turn away, but I was entranced.

"Can I have a word with you in private?"

I hesitated, afraid that if I stood, he'd see the imprint of my half-hard cock against the soft fabric of the sweatpants. But in the end, the desire to spend more time with him won out. "Okay."

"Good." He gave a small smile and straightened to address the others. "Do you two mind leaving Milo and me alone to speak?"

The stool beside me moved as Danny got off and shifted away. Presumably, Melinda followed, but I was unable to tear my gaze from Everett. The other man's nostrils flared and a muscle in his jaw ticked.

"You really don't make this easy," he grumbled.

I frowned, confused. "What's wrong?"

"Nothing." He cleared his throat. "Well, actually, there is something. We can't find Tomas. My brother, the sheriff, checked his record. The guy has a history of violence against omegas."

"He does?" My stomach tightened. I felt sick knowing what a narrow escape I'd had, and I couldn't bring myself to ask what he'd done in the past because I didn't want to know what fate I'd escaped that other poor omegas might not have.

"Yes, and because you got away from him, there's a chance he might come after you. We'd like you to stay here, with Momma, until we track him down. Just to be on the safe side."

"No." I was already shaking my head. "I've imposed on

Melinda enough. I don't want to put her out, and I'm sure I'll be fine." I always had been before.

"I'd really like it if you stayed," he said, placing his hand on the center of the counter, palm up, as though giving me the opportunity to take his hand.

I hesitated, unsure how to respond. The sensible thing would be to get back to my normal life—including the job I couldn't afford to lose—as soon as possible. "I shouldn't."

"Please." His voice was soft. "I won't be comfortable knowing you're out there on your own when you might be in danger."

Everything inside me melted. Something I hadn't felt for a long time began to unfurl in my gut. Hope. Could Everett really care for me? He barely knew me. Was this some kind of white knight complex? I'd been looking after myself for long enough that I didn't need a knight to save me. Although sometimes, in my darkest moments, I thought it might be nice to have one anyway.

"Stay," Everett urged.

"Okay," I whispered, placing my hand on his. I'd wait until they'd tracked down Tomas and then go on my way. I could make myself useful in the meantime, so I wouldn't be too much of an imposition. "I'll call my boss to ask for a couple of days off work."

Everett intertwined our fingers and a beautiful warmth filled me that I'd never experienced before. "Make it a week."

CHAPTER
SIX

EVERETT

Once Milo had made the call to his boss, I excused myself from the kitchen, gesturing for Momma and Danny to go back in. Momma did, but Danny followed me out through the front door. He'd probably caught a glimpse of my eyes, which had shifted. Or perhaps my fangs, which kept dropping every time I scented Milo. My bear wanted to claim him. So did I. But the sweet omega didn't even know shifters existed, so I couldn't just jump him the way I wanted.

"He's your mate?" Danny asked once the door had closed behind us.

I grunted an affirmation.

"He's cute," Danny said. "Gorgeous eyes, and he has this whole quiet and mysterious thing going on."

I growled, my bear instinctively reacting to Danny's words even though it was ridiculous. They were both omegas. The chance of Danny being interested in him was minuscule, yet I felt the need to defend my claim.

"Whoa, now." Danny held up his hand in a gesture of peace. "I don't want your man."

I scowled because who wouldn't want Milo? He was perfect.

"Okay, poor word choice," Danny said with a sigh. "You've always been a grump, but you're not usually so temperamental."

I winced. "Sorry, he brings it out in me."

He smiled, his expression a little wistful. "It's nice." The smile fell away. "So, how did you know he was your mate?"

I glanced toward the house to make sure nobody would be able to overhear us. "His scent. He smelled of cherries, and it called to me. I knew before I even saw him that he was my mate."

"That sounds wonderful." Danny's shoulders slumped, and I wondered if he was thinking about his last boyfriend. The alpha that had abused him. I wished, once again, that he had come to me or one of our brothers and asked for help before the day I'd walked into his house and found him getting beat to a pulp. For some reason, he hadn't thought he could talk to us about it, and that haunted me. I'd failed to protect him when he needed it. What kind of alpha did that make me?

Now, Milo needed protection. I prayed to the Gods that I didn't let him down too. I wouldn't be able to live with myself if I did.

"So, what are you going to do about him?" Danny asked, breaking my train of thought.

"Hell if I know." In all my daydreams about what my mate might be like, I'd never imagined them being clueless about our world. I'd thought we'd meet one day and fall into each other's arms. But that wasn't normal human behavior, and I couldn't expect it from Milo. "I guess I'll have to ask him out. Not yet though. He's still recovering from his last date." My jaw clenched. If I found Tomas, I was going to make him pay for frightening Milo so badly.

"In the meantime, do you think you could try not to scare him off? I don't want to overwhelm him. You know our family can be a lot."

Danny grinned. "I'll try not to, but I think you underestimate him. Besides, maybe he likes big, crazy families. Some people do."

"I guess we'll find out."

~

THAT NIGHT, I went to Dad and Momma's place for dinner, knowing that all of my brothers would be there too most likely. Usually we ate at the family home a couple of nights a week, but no doubt they'd all be curious to see more of Milo. I was the first one of us to have found their mate, and they'd want to learn all they could about him. We were that kind of family. Zander, especially, would be curious, as he hadn't seen Milo yet.

Hearing voices inside, I jogged up the front steps. I could make out Dad's, Momma's, and Danny's, but I didn't hear Milo. That didn't surprise me. From what I'd discovered about my mate so far, he wasn't the gregarious type. I strode down the hall and into the dining room, following my nose. It smelled as though Momma had been cooking up a storm. Several covered platters and dishes sat in the center of the dining table, and Momma, Dad, Danny, and Milo were arranged around one end of it.

Milo looked up as I entered and his eyes drank me in. My chest puffed out, my bear pleased that our mate seemed to like what he saw.

"Everett."

I dropped into a chair to hide the way my cock plumped when he said my name in that breathy voice. "How are you feeling?"

"I'm good." The corners of his mouth lifted enough that I was reasonably sure he was being honest. He started to say something else, but heavy footsteps thumped up the hall behind me, signaling the arrival of one of my brothers. I tried to tamp down my frustration at the interruption. I wanted to know what Milo had to say.

Garrick burst into the room, with Zander close behind him. Garrick came to an abrupt halt, and Zander crashed into his back.

"Hello." Garrick smiled at Milo. "Do you remember me?"

Milo shook his head, his eyes wide. I got the impression he hadn't been expecting to see them. Perhaps Momma hadn't warned him he'd likely be ambushed tonight.

"My name is Garrick." Garrick crossed over to him and held out a hand, which Milo took but released quickly. My bear purred in approval. Only I got to hold his hand. "I was with Everett when he found you in the woods. We work on the same search and rescue team."

"Garrick is my boss," I told Milo.

"Nice to meet you properly." Milo's earlier smile had vanished. He seemed tense. "Thank you for rescuing me."

Garrick shrugged. "Just doing my job. I'm glad you're all right."

Zander stepped around Garrick to greet Milo. "I'm Zander. I'm the oldest brother."

Milo glanced at his uniform. "You're the sheriff?"

Zander nodded. "Yes."

"Oh." He gulped, and I wondered if he'd had run-ins with law enforcement in the past. Surely not. He was too sweet for that. "Nice to meet you."

Momma gestured for Zander and Garrick to sit. "Dig in," she said.

We all reached for the food. Out of the corner of my eye,

I watched Milo sitting back, apparently scared to enter the fray. Hardly surprising, considering the entire family ate like the ravenous bears we were. I grabbed his plate and piled steamed vegetables, potatoes, and venison onto it, then offered it to him.

He smiled appreciatively. "Thanks."

"No problem."

The family chatted while we ate. Every now and then, Danny or Momma would ask Milo a question, trying to draw him into the conversation. I noticed that he didn't seem to like being put on the spot, so I glared at Danny and gestured for him to knock it off. My mate would open up in his own time. I kept an eye on Milo, as much because I simply couldn't take my eyes off him than for any other reason. He ate less than us, but for a human, he was fast to shovel food into his mouth. It made me wonder if there had been times in the past when he'd gone hungry. Fuck, I hated that idea.

Protect, my bear grumbled.

Yes, I agreed. Milo would never go without again. We wouldn't allow it.

When the meal ended, Milo volunteered to wash up.

"You don't have to do that," Momma protested. "You're our guest."

He raised his chin. "I'd really like to. You cooked such a delicious meal, and I want to contribute."

"I'll help," I said, shoving my chair out and standing before Momma could argue. "Come on, Milo."

We gathered the dirty dishes and I guided him to the kitchen and turned on the tap to fill the sink. "The dish towels are in the third drawer down," I said, waving a hand in the general direction.

Milo got a towel and joined me as I started scrubbing the plates. We worked in companionable silence. As we were nearing the end, I passed him a pot and our fingers brushed. A thrill of attraction jolted through me, setting my nerves alight and instantly making me hard. Before I had time to think, I found myself in front of Milo, pressing him against the kitchen counter. I stared down at his lips, mesmerized by them. I needed to taste him. But when I raised my eyes, I saw uncertainty flash across his features.

Shit.

The poor guy had just been attacked, and here I was, manhandling him. I dropped my hands from his hips and backed away.

"I'm so sorry." I turned tail and fled.

CHAPTER

SEVEN

MILO
I gazed out the door Everett had exited through, wondering what had caused him to run like that. He'd been about to kiss me, hadn't he? It had happened quickly, but I could have sworn I felt his erection press against me and that there had been desire in his eyes. Had I misunderstood?

Heart sinking, I put away the last of the dishes and returned to the dining room, only to find it nearly empty. Only Aaron, Melinda's husband, remained at his seat, drinking whiskey.

He set it down and glanced up at me. "Come and sit with me. Would you like a drink?"

I hesitated, not really wanting to be alone with him, but Aaron gave off such an air of authority that I felt like I had no choice. I took the seat opposite and, when he poured a finger of whiskey into another glass and pushed it across the table, I sipped. The stuff was strong.

"You must be worn out after the past two days," he said, sympathy in his voice.

"Yes, sir." I was exhausted. My escapade in the woods

had been traumatic enough. Waking up in an unfamiliar place, surrounded by people I didn't know, and finding out that Tomas might come after me again had frayed my edges. I liked routine. Predictability. This was anything but.

"I'm sorry for what you've been through." He leaned toward me, his eyes locked on mine. He possessed the same unnerving intensity as Everett. "I hope you know that not all of us who live in the area are disrespectful cretins who don't know that no means no."

"I do." I pretended to drink more of the whiskey, but I didn't want to be at anything less than my best because I didn't understand where Aaron was going with this conversation. He must have a point, or he wouldn't have invited me to join him, and he wouldn't be watching me so intently. "You've all been very kind. I really appreciate your hospitality."

He waved his hand dismissively. "Don't thank me for maintaining a basic level of human decency. It should be what you expect."

I glanced at the tabletop, determined not to meet his gaze, because in my experience, expecting a basic level of decency was often asking too much. The places I'd been and the homes I'd lived in had taught me not to trust anyone. Especially not a stranger.

"I'd like to know more about you." He straightened. "Melinda says you're from Grayton."

I nodded. "That's right."

"What do you do there?" he asked.

"I'm an accountant." Hopefully that would put an end to his questions. Nobody found accountants interesting, but it was a stable job that allowed me to keep a small apartment all of my own, and after years without a home, that was worth more than gold.

"Very good." He smiled, and for some reason the

approval in his expression eased my nerves. "Do you live downtown?"

"Yes, sir. I have an apartment."

"Alone?"

I cocked my head. Was he trying to figure out if anyone would miss me?

Don't be crazy.

"I have a roommate. Steve." Technically, Steve was a succulent. But he did share the apartment with me, and it made me feel safer to stretch the truth so he wouldn't realize I could vanish off the face of the earth and no one but my boss would care. Not that I thought Aaron was a serial killer or anything, but it was better to be safe than sorry.

"Just a roommate?" he asked. "Not a boyfriend?"

I laughed. "Definitely not. Besides, if he were, I'd hardly have been out with Tomas, would I?"

"Good point." His face relaxed. Until then, I hadn't realized how much tension he'd been holding.

I yawned, and made a point of emphasizing it. "I'm tired."

Aaron tossed back the last of his whiskey. "Go get some sleep, Milo. You're safe here."

My eyes widened in surprise. Had he been able to see my discomfort? How embarrassing. "Um, thank you."

I stood and excused myself, hoping he wouldn't notice that I'd barely touched the whiskey. In the hall, I almost collided with Danny, who was coming the other way.

"Oh, hey." Danny grabbed my shoulders to steady me. "Where are you running away to in such a hurry?"

He glanced back into the dining room. "Ah. Gotcha. Dad can be a bit intimidating."

"He's fine," I mumbled. "I'd, uh, better get to bed or I'll fall over soon."

"Hold on a moment." He removed his hands from my shoulders and moved closer, speaking quietly. "Did I see you and Everett kissing in the kitchen?"

My face flamed. "No."

"Really?" He actually looked disappointed. "I could have sworn…"

I shrugged. "Nope. We did the dishes and then he raced out. Maybe he had to be somewhere." I didn't want to admit that I suspected the only place Everett needed to be was away from me. "Besides, Everett is way out of my league. There's no way anything is happening there."

Danny arched an eyebrow. "You are so clueless. It's adorable."

"Hey!"

"Don't take offense." He touched my arm. "Trust me when I say that Everett likes you. Unfortunately, Ev doesn't date much so you'll have to be patient with him. If you do, I promise he'll be worth it."

"I don't date much either," I admitted. "Last time I did, you know what happened."

He cringed. "Not great. But Everett won't be like that. Just give him a chance."

My heart skipped. He really believed that his brother was interested in me. I could hardly credit it. Everett was strong and rugged and gorgeous. I was just me. Too small, too quiet, too boring for anyone to notice.

"I think you've read the situation completely wrong," I told him. "But if Everett were to ask me out, I'd say yes and see how it went. Happy?"

He grinned. "Ecstatic." He kissed my cheek and ruffled my hair. "Off to bed with you. You'll feel much better after another good sleep."

I ducked away from him, trying to hide how pleased I was by his obvious affection even though we hardly knew each other. Touch-starved. I was so touch-starved. "Night-night."

"Sleep tight," he called after me.

I headed to the spare bedroom, shaking my head. What kind of bizarre place had I landed in?

CHAPTER

EIGHT

EVERETT

After leaving Dad and Momma's place, I shifted and ran through the woods behind my home until my bear was exhausted, then limped home, showered, and fell into bed. Unfortunately, I couldn't sleep. Despite being bone-tired, I craved my mate too badly to surrender to oblivion. I was hard, and even when I jacked off it did little to relieve my need for him. In the early hours of the morning, after catching only a few brief snatches of rest, I gave up and made myself coffee, then decided to check whether there was any sign the wolf had been in the area.

I left my clothes folded on the back porch and shifted. I circled my parents' place first, eager to ensure there was no evidence that our enemy had been anywhere near my mate. I was relieved not to smell the wolf. That done, I padded into the woods and made my way around the town's perimeter. As I drew near the main road into Grizzly Ridge, I caught the scent of wet fur carried on the breeze and froze. It was faint, but the wolf had been here. Perhaps a couple of hours ago.

I followed the scent, tracing a path between the trees

until we reached the road, where the trail abruptly vanished. Perhaps he'd gotten into a car and driven away. Whatever the case, he'd been sniffing around Milo, and that wasn't acceptable. I raced back to my place, donned my clothes, and walked the short distance to my parents' house. It was still early. A little after dawn, if I had to guess, but Dad would be awake. He only slept a few hours a night.

Instead of knocking, I grabbed the spare key from inside one of the shoes lined up beside the door and let myself in. I headed straight for the kitchen, knowing Dad would likely be drinking coffee at the breakfast bar, enjoying the solitude before anyone else turned up. Sure enough, he sat behind the counter with a mug of coffee off to the side and the newspaper spread out in front of him. He looked up and nodded in welcome.

"There's more coffee in the pot," he said.

"Thanks." I poured myself a cup and sat beside him. "I ran a circuit around town. Smelled wolf."

He frowned. "The same one?"

"Hard to say. I didn't pay much attention to his scent the last time, but this scent definitely came from a lone wolf."

"Hmm." He pursed his lips, and I knew him well enough to see that he was worried. We didn't need other shifters moving into our clan's territory—especially not renegades or rogue packs. "How much have you heard about the pack in Moonlight Cove?"

I shrugged. "Only what Garrick told me. They haven't done much damage yet."

He nodded. "Technically that's true, but I heard from Renny, who runs the tavern there, that they treat the local omegas poorly and have terrified a couple of human tourists. From what Renny said there are at least six of them, and so far they haven't caused enough problems for anyone to raise the alarm to neighboring shifter groups, but Renny has a bad feeling about them, and so do I."

I took a mouthful of coffee, mulling over his words. Dad was wise. It was the reason he'd been a good Alpha for so many years. If he was concerned, then I would be too. "You think the lone wolf is one from the pack?"

He turned toward me. "It makes sense. It would be a strange coincidence if a lone wolf showed up at the same time as a rogue pack moved into the area."

"It would be," I agreed. "Whoever he is, if he tries to touch my omega again, I'll rip him apart."

Some of the tension lifted from Dad's face. "So, he's definitely yours, then?"

"Yeah." I grinned. "Not that he knows it yet."

"Give him time, son. I get the impression that the young man hasn't had an easy life."

"I will." I got the same impression, and it made me want to bury whoever had treated him badly. I stiffened and pricked my ears, hearing footfalls in the hall. A moment later, a bleary-eyed Milo wandered into the kitchen wearing a pair of my old pajamas. My dick thickened and pressed against the zipper of my jeans. Damn, he looked good in my clothes. I wanted to rip them off him and worship his body, or cover him in my scent so all other alphas knew he was off-limits. I felt my eyes change and my fangs drop. I stared down at the counter, hoping Milo wouldn't see them.

"Good morning," he said hesitantly.

I grunted, afraid that if I tried to speak, my words would be distorted by my fangs and he'd notice. He took a step back and his scent changed, telling me he was nervous. Fucking hell. Was I doomed to constantly screw up when it came to this omega?

CHAPTER

NINE

MILO

I kept my mouth shut as I poured coffee and found the bread Melinda had told me to use for breakfast. I didn't know what I'd done to upset Everett, but considering he'd run away from me yesterday and was barely speaking to me this morning, it must have been something.

"How did you sleep?" Aaron asked, his tone more welcoming than Everett's.

"Very good, thank you." The bed was a dream. Seriously. I'd never slept on anything so comfortable in my life.

I put bread in the toaster.

"You have everything you need?" Aaron asked. "I hope Melinda made it clear you're welcome to anything. We want you to be at home here."

I nodded and sent him a quick smile. "She's been very kind."

Melinda was everything I thought a mother should be, and seeing the relationship between her and her sons last night, I'd felt a fierce longing to experience that kind of

44

affection and acceptance myself. Unfortunately, I never would. The fantasy was one that was doomed to be unfulfilled.

When the toast popped, I spread honey onto it from a huge container in the pantry—seriously, who needed so much honey?—and ate quickly. Both men seemed content to let me have my breakfast in peace, which I was grateful for because it meant I could make a quick getaway. I couldn't handle being around Everett for longer than necessary, knowing I'd messed up somehow. As soon as I was done, I washed my plate and cup and excused myself, but as I made for the exit, Everett stopped me with a hand on my forearm.

"Wait," he said. "Can we talk outside?"

My shoulders drew up to my ears. So much for a quick escape. "Sure."

He put his hand on my lower back to guide me to the door and fizzles of electricity hummed through me from his touch. I'd never experienced animal attraction before, but I felt it now, and it was annoyingly inconvenient. Why couldn't I have this reaction to a guy who wouldn't flee rather than go through the horror of kissing me?

Everett led me onto the front porch and stopped. "Are you okay?" he asked. "Something is off. You seem upset."

"Me?" My eyes widened. Was he serious?

"Yes. Tell me what it is so I can fix it."

My eyebrows drew together. That didn't sound like a man who didn't want to be near me. I was so confused. "I'm fine," I told him. "But you're acting like you're upset or angry with me, and I don't know what I did."

"No, baby." Surprise flashed through his eyes. Perhaps the endearment had just slipped out. "You did nothing wrong. You're absolutely perfect." He reached for my hand

and clasped it between both of his. "I'm just working through some things, but I promise, anger is the last thing I feel when it comes to you. Unless it's about that asshole who tried to hurt you." Something dangerous crossed his face and I shivered.

I studied him carefully as I mulled over what he'd said. It sounded like a whole lot of 'it's not you, it's me' bullshit, but those intense eyes of his seemed too open and vulnerable for him to be messing with me. Was it possible he meant it? A thread of excitement wormed into my gut, but I tried not to let it grow. The last thing I needed was to get my hopes up for nothing.

"Do you believe me?" he asked, his eyes silently begging me to agree.

I let out a long breath. "I do."

Even if I didn't understand it.

"That's good." He ducked his head and brushed his lips over my cheek. They were softer than I would have guessed, with a faint rasp from his beard. "I have to go now. I have work to do. Make sure you keep someone with you all day. I need you to be safe."

I nodded because what else was I going to do? It wasn't as if I planned to wander through the woods on my own. No, thank you. Not after what I'd been through.

"I'll see you later, then."

"Goodbye." I watched him go, my gaze dropping to his muscular, round ass. The man filled out a pair of jeans very nicely.

I returned inside. Aaron was no longer in the kitchen, but Melinda was. She was singing to herself, an apron wrapped around her waist, as she removed baking ingredients from the pantry and placed them on the kitchen counter. Flour. Cocoa. Vanilla extract. Something else I didn't recognize. I approached slowly, not wanting to startle her.

"Hello, Melinda."

"Hi, darling." She glanced over her shoulder and flashed me a smile. "Was that Everett leaving?"

"Yes."

She tutted. "That man needs an omega to make sure he gets a good night's sleep. I bet he's been up for hours already."

I looked down, praying she wouldn't notice the way my cheeks heated at her mention of Everett having an omega. I wanted that job, but despite our conversation outside, I still didn't know where we stood. He'd told me I was perfect, but he hadn't said he wanted to date me. Even if he did, my life was in the city and his was here. How could it work?

"What are you baking?" I asked, needing a distraction.

"Muffins and bread for the children's home." She opened a drawer and grabbed a stack of bowls. "I try to bring them something a few times a week."

My stomach squeezed. "There's a local home?"

I would have thought Grizzly Ridge was too small for that. Not that I'd seen much of the town beyond this house.

As if reading my mind, she said, "The home takes children from all the surrounding towns. Many of them have nowhere else to go."

I felt sick. The memories of my own time in group homes were fresh despite how many years had passed. I'd always been small and weak, and some of the bigger children had picked on me. Then, as I'd gotten older, another type of danger had appeared. A more ominous one. While I hadn't been assaulted as many other homeless girls and omegas were, it had been a close call. One of the boys who'd been about to age out of the system had gotten his eye on me, and it was only through a lucky interruption that he hadn't had the chance to hurt me.

Melinda must have read my expression because she wrapped me in a hug. "Oh, honey. They're well cared for, I promise. The whole community contributes to make sure those kids have as much as we can give them."

I buried my face against her soft form, drinking in the comfort. The thing she couldn't understand was that no matter how much stuff those kids had, it wouldn't make up for a lack of affection from a parental figure like her. At least they weren't going hungry though. I knew from experience how awful that was.

I pulled back and forced myself not to fall apart. "Can I help?" My voice was shakier than I'd have liked, but Melinda didn't comment on it. "I love to bake, and I'd like to do something for the kids."

"Of course." She gestured toward a battered cookbook on the counter. "The recipes are over there. Why don't you make a start on the muffins and I'll do the bread?"

"That would be great." Bread was more difficult to make than muffins, and it was something I hadn't perfected yet. In general, I'd done more cooking than baking, putting together whatever I could out of the few things in the pantry at the home I was in at the time. Baking meant having ingredients, and that wasn't a luxury I'd been able to indulge in until I'd started working. "Thank you."

She put a hand on her hip and narrowed her eyes. "Milo, if you tell me 'thank you' one more time, I might have to spank you with a spatula. You're our guest and we like having you here. You don't have to be so darned grateful."

"Okay." I stared at her, eyes wide. "Th—" I caught myself. "I'll start on these muffins."

"You do that." She smiled and patted my shoulder.

I found the recipe and checked through the ingredients on the counter. She already had everything we needed, so I began putting them together in the order the recipe advised.

"So," Melinda said after a few minutes. "That was quite a reaction you had before. Am I right in thinking you have personal experience with a children's home?"

I bit my lip, cursing myself for making her curious. "Yes, I grew up in group homes and foster homes."

"I'm sorry, darling. What happened to your parents?"

My shoulders stiffened but I kept working, cracking eggs into a hollow in the center of the dry ingredients. "I don't know. They're either dead or they didn't want me. I was in the system from birth."

I heard a quick intake of breath but didn't look at her. If she felt sorry for me, I couldn't bear to see it. "That's terrible. And you didn't get adopted?"

"No." It had almost happened once. I'd been so hopeful that the couple would take me away from a life of constant moving and hunger, but they'd finally had their own biological child after years of trying and had decided they didn't want me after all. "How many children are in the local home?" I asked to divert the conversation away from my past.

"There must be eight or so at the moment." She hummed in thought. "Would you like to come with me when I take the food over? I'm sure the children would love to meet you. After all, you've been in their shoes and made something of yourself."

Pride surged through me. I *had* made something of myself. I wasn't rich or famous, but I'd managed to get a degree and a steady job, and now I always knew that I'd have a paycheck coming and enough food to see me through. Not to mention a roof over my head that wasn't leaky or infested with rats. But much as I'd like to give hope to those kids, I couldn't go back to a group home. There was every chance I'd break down in tears, and that was hardly going to help them.

"Not today," I said, realizing she was waiting for a response. "Maybe next time." If there was one. It wasn't as if I'd be in town for much longer.

EVERETT

I knocked on Zander's office door and opened it when he grunted a welcome.

"Any sign of the wolf?" I asked, leaning against the door frame.

He scowled. "None. I've spoken to the Alpha of the rogue pack, and he says Tomas is one of theirs but they haven't seen him in the past couple of days. He might be lurking in the area to stalk Milo."

It was my turn to scowl. "Damn. I guess it's too much to ask that they do something about it?"

"It didn't sound like he planned to act."

I growled under my breath. "Why do you think Tomas is so fixated on Milo?"

Zander shrugged. "Milo said the guy tried to bite him. Maybe he legitimately believes that Milo is his fated mate."

"He's not," I snapped. "That bastard is nothing to him, and if he tries to come near him, I'll tear him apart."

Zander's expression grew pained. "I wish you wouldn't threaten to break the law where I can hear you. Vent outside if you need to, but at least give me plausible deniability."

I shook my head. "Just wait until you find an omega. You wouldn't be so calm if it were your mate in danger."

Zander's eyes flashed to his bear. "I hope you're not suggesting that I'm not taking Milo's predicament seriously."

"No, of course not." I knew he was taking whatever steps he could, short of assigning constant surveillance, which the sheriff's department would barely have the resources for anyway. "I'm just frustrated. I want Milo to be in the clear so I can woo the shit out of him and figure out how the hell I'm supposed to tell him that I have a furry alter ego."

Zander's face relaxed into a grin. "Can't help you there. I've never had to break the news to someone before. But just a suggestion: try to be tactful. Use your words. Don't just shift in front of him or the poor guy will have another date from hell to add to his list."

"Tactful." I tugged at the ends of my hair. "That's not really my thing, brother."

"This time, it needs to be."

I nodded. He was right. My usual blunt approach wouldn't be the way to win Milo over. "I'll see you later. I'm going home to my mate."

Zander's lips twitched. "You're just saying it to rub it in that you have one."

"Nah." I raised a hand in farewell. "I like the way it sounds."

I did love it. Milo was mine, and knowing that was pretty incredible. I'd had no idea what my mate would be like—if I ever found them—but Milo was everything I wanted wrapped up in a beguilingly shy package.

I headed home, my mind full of images of Milo's face.

I'd been storing them each time I saw him. The way his eyebrows pinched when he was worried, and how his smile seemed to appear against his will. I'd have to earn every one of them, and I relished the challenge. But first I'd have to stop putting my foot in my mouth.

I was so distracted that I almost didn't notice the foreign scent until I reached my parents' front door. I froze, my nostrils flaring as I inhaled the muskiness of wolf. It was the same scent I'd noticed earlier. Tomas had been here. I spun around, half-expecting to find him behind me, but nothing was there. I breathed in again, trying to gauge how fresh the scent was. I'd guess he'd been here within the hour. Unless he was still lurking in the shadows or behind a building.

I unlocked the door and bolted inside, following the delicious scent of cherries until I found Milo in the spare bedroom, staring out the window with his knees to his chest.

"Thank Gods," I breathed.

He flinched and his head turned my way. "You scared me."

His eyes were wide and wary. I never wanted to see them that way again.

"Shh, it's just me." I sat on the edge of the bed and reached for his hand, but he drew it away. "Where's Momma?"

"In the kitchen." He looked confused. "What's wrong?"

"Tomas has been here."

He paled. "What? How do you know?"

"I just do. Trust me." I could hardly explain that I'd smelled him. At least, not yet. That could wait until after Milo had warmed up to me more. "He could still be in the area. You need to make sure you have someone with you at all times."

His chin thrust forward. "She's right down the hall," he said defensively.

"It's not enough." My bear was seething and desperate to get to the surface. He wanted to hunt down the wolf and end him. "I want someone in the same room as you."

"Surely that's overkill." He grimaced. "It's not like there's anything special about me. He'll probably get tired of scaring me after a day and leave."

"What do you mean there's nothing special about you?" I demanded. My omega was brilliant. Beautiful. So damn brave for the way he'd gotten away from the wolf and kept himself safe. "Never mind, we'll deal with that later." For now, I needed to get him to take me seriously. "Please, Milo. Promise me." I scooted closer and cupped his face with one hand. "I'd go fucking crazy if anything happened to you."

His eyes heated as they held mine, and I caught a glimpse of the desire I'd seen in him before. His pink lips parted.

God, those lips. I had to taste them. Just a little. One kiss wouldn't hurt.

I lowered my mouth to his.

CHAPTER
ELEVEN

MILO

Everett's kiss was everything I'd imagined. Soft and sensual at first, but it grew bolder with every passing second. His tongue swooped into my mouth and suddenly his flavor swamped my senses. He tasted of honey. I never knew that could be an aphrodisiac, but it was.

A whimper escaped me. Embarrassment flared at my lack of control, but then Everett groaned and yanked me closer, cradling me on his lap. He plundered my mouth, stealing my breath and my ability to think about anything other than the sensation of his rough palm on my cheek and the contrast between the satin of his lips and the rasp of his beard.

Wait. Hold on.

I pulled back, and with a burst of willpower detached my lips from his. I dipped my chin, determined not to look at his face while I caught my breath. "What was that?" I demanded. "And what do you mean, you'd go crazy if anything happened to me? I don't get you. One moment I think you're interested in me, and the next I have no idea what you think of me."

"I know, baby."

He tried to tuck me beneath his chin but I resisted, needing to be able to see his face so I at least stood a chance of telling whether he was being honest with me. His gaze traveled to my mouth again, and he licked his lips. My cock jerked, but I ignored that traitor. I needed answers, damn it.

"I'm sorry for sending you mixed signals." He raised my hand to his lips and kissed it. The gentle touch sent a frisson of awareness shooting through me. Butterflies threw a rave in my tummy. Why did he have to be so swoony?

"The truth is, I like you, and I want you, but you just went through something difficult and you deserve time to recover."

I frowned, studying his expression. It looked honest enough. Some of my righteous anger faded. "Seriously? That's what this is about?"

He hesitated for just long enough to make me wonder, then nodded.

"Isn't it up to me to decide what I want and when I'm ready for it?" I asked. "We do live in the age of omega equality, you know."

His lips twitched. "What do you want, baby?"

My insides melted. I had to admit that I loved it when he called me "baby." No one ever had before. I used to think it was cheesy when guys did that, but it made me feel cherished.

"I'd like some more of those kisses, to start with."

His lips curved in a slow smile. "Your wish is my command."

In that moment, I could almost imagine that this alpha was, indeed, mine to command. But that was a fantasy.

Alphas didn't let omegas call the shots. Especially not strong, confident ones like Everett. Yet as he claimed my mouth, I believed it. A rumble rolled through him, coming from deep in his chest, and a thrill of power skittered through my veins. I'd made him react like that. Me.

Without taking my mouth from his, I repositioned myself, straddling his legs. His hardness brushed against mine and I moaned and rocked my hips, rubbing myself against the ridge.

"That's it, baby." He gripped my ass and spoke against my lips. "Take what you need."

I rolled my hips again and my head fell back when pleasure roared through me. I was so close. So close to coming. I'd never been intimate with another person before, but I was pretty sure it was supposed to take longer than this and I didn't want to shoot like a virgin during his first time. Even if, technically, I was.

"Need to slow down," I murmured.

Everett stiffened and removed his hands from me. "Sorry." His voice was a rasp. "Didn't mean to rush you. Shit. You okay?"

I whimpered, hating the sense of distance between us. "Yes, I didn't mean stop. I just don't want to come too fast."

"Oh." A wicked smile stole over his face. His hands returned to my ass and he kissed up the side of my neck, pausing to gently bite on the space where it joined my shoulder. "God, you make me crazy."

"That's good, right?" I couldn't help the sudden bout of insecurity.

"Fuck, yeah." He stopped toying with my neck and looked at me, staring right into my eyes so fiercely I nearly looked away. "Milo," he said tentatively. "Have you been with a man before?"

My cheeks heated, and I shook my head. His eyes

flashed, and for a second, I could have sworn they'd changed from brown to gold. Did he wear contacts? I'd have to ask later.

He released a shuddering sigh. "I don't know how I got so lucky."

"You don't mind?" I knew some alphas preferred omegas with experience.

His eyes did that strange flashy thing again. "I love the fact that no one else has ever touched you like this. If I get my way, they never will."

I shivered. Perhaps the possessive statement should be a red flag, but it wasn't. For so long, I'd wanted to be some-one's first choice. The person they most cared about. And him offering me a chance at that? It was too good to be true.

I kissed him. "I want that too. Now, hurry up and touch me again." Our brief exchange had cooled my ardor.

Everett slid a hand down my abdomen, to the front of my sweats, and cupped my dick. "Is this okay?"

"More than."

He eased his fingers beneath the waistband and stilled, obviously realizing I wasn't wearing underwear. I hadn't wanted to borrow any, and my own was in the laundry. He curled his fingers around my shaft and stroked. A whimper tore from me and my eyes fluttered shut.

"Look at me," he ordered.

Fighting against the wave of pleasure as he stroked me again, I opened my eyes and tried to focus on his.

"Good, baby. I need to see those gorgeous eyes."

He gathered my precum and used it as lube to ease the movement of his palm as he started to jack me off. I pressed my lips to his, my hips rolling, thrusting into his fist, never letting my eyes close. Hot approval simmered in Everett's golden eyes. One of his teeth nicked my lip but his tongue soothed the spot instantly. My cock throbbed, and I pulled away from him, struggling to breathe as pleasure crept up my spine and threatened to overwhelm me. My forehead hit his shoulder, but then he removed the hand from my ass and used it to tilt my chin up.

"Open," he growled.

I blinked at him, my vision hazy. "Ev. I need. Oh, God. I need."

"I know what you need." He added a twist to his jerking motion and wrapped his other hand around my throat. Not squeezing, or even putting pressure on it. Just maintaining a steady, commanding grip.

"Oh, fuck. I'm coming." I cried out as I came, my release splattering over his shirt and coating his hand. He eased me through it, and as I stopped shuddering, he licked my come off his hand, never breaking eye contact with me. My cock pulsed again, and another spurt of come landed on his stomach. He drew me forward and kissed me. I could taste myself on him. Oh, God. That was filthy. So fucking filthy. I loved it.

"How do you feel?" he asked.

"Amazing," I whispered. As I returned to earth, I realized I could still feel the rock-hard outline of his erection beneath me. I wriggled off him, tore off my shirt so I wouldn't spread come anywhere, and stared at his crotch. "Can I?"

He watched me intently, his nostrils flaring, and gave a slight nod. With trembling fingers, I undid the button of his fly and tugged the zipper down. I'd never given a blow job before, but I wanted to make him feel the way he'd made me feel. More than that, I wanted to taste him. He raised his hips and pushed his jeans down, so he was left in his underwear. My eyes widened as I took him in. I'd been able to tell he was large, but he was even bigger than I'd guessed, and based on the wet patch soaking through the fabric, he was riding the edge.

Instinct made me lower myself onto my belly and bury my face between his thighs. I inhaled, loving the musky scent of him. Everett growled, and even though I was the one preparing to go down on him, I'd never felt so powerful. I peeled his underwear back to reveal his long, thick cock. It was smooth and heavy, the head red and slick with precum. I touched my tongue to the tip to taste him. Salty.

"Oh, fuck." He groaned. "Milo. Baby. Are you sure?"

"Yes." I wanted that beautiful dick in my mouth. I'd never been more certain of anything. I shoved his underwear beneath his balls and cupped them in my palm. They were full, tight, and lightly furred. "I love these." I nuzzled them, then I circled his cock with my thumb and forefinger —which didn't even come close to closing around him— and took the head between my lips. I swirled my tongue around the silken head, cleaning up the precum and learning his texture.

He shuddered, and his fingers delved into my hair. "Please, baby. Don't tease me. I need you too badly."

I was teasing? Huh.

Smiling to myself, I allowed his shaft to rest on the flat of my tongue and swallowed him down as deep as I could. Considering his size and my inexperience, it wasn't as far as I'd have liked, but he groaned and the muscles of his abdomen rippled as though he was barely holding himself back. Another thrill ran through me. I loved the thought of him overpowering me and taking what he wanted. But maybe another day. When we knew each other better.

I set my mind to pleasing him, sucking and licking with everything I had, determined that even if it wasn't the best blow job he'd ever had, it would be the most enthusiastic.

"That's so good, baby." His fingers ran through my hair

and cupped the back of my head. "Fuck." He hissed between his teeth and gave a slight thrust into my mouth. My eyes watered, but I liked the burn, so I grabbed his butt and encouraged him to do it again. His cock thickened in my mouth, stretching my lips obscenely. "I'm gonna come. Pull off if you need."

Something fluttered in my heart. Even as he was losing control, he was thinking of me. I redoubled my efforts, and when he roared my name and shot into my mouth, I drank as much of his seed as I could, gathering anything that leaked out the corners of my mouth and licking it up as he watched with hooded eyes.

"My omega," he rasped, and hauled me up his body, holding me against his chest, mindless of the mess between us. "Mine."

"Yes, alpha." I rested my cheek over his heart and listened to the rapid thump. If this was a dream, I never wanted it to end. "Yours."

He dipped his head and seemed to sniff me.

I giggled. "Is there something in the water around here that makes men like to sniff people?"

He rolled his eyes and kissed my forehead softly. "No, little one. You just smell so good that everyone wants a piece of you."

CHAPTER

TWELVE

EVERETT

Being mated to a human was the most frustrating thing I'd ever experienced and simultaneously the most wonderful. I adored Milo already, but sleeping curled around him without being able to sink my teeth into him and claim him as mine challenged every ounce of my self-control.

When I woke, wrapped in sleepy omega, his scent enveloping me, I'd had to get out of there. I'd kissed his forehead and left a note on the nightstand so he'd know I didn't regret what we'd done and then headed to the bakery to talk it over with Danny. Neither Garrick nor Zander would be any help. Danny might laugh at me, but at least he was an omega and could offer advice that wouldn't be terrible. My alpha brothers—Garrick in particular—had no trouble getting omegas to fall into bed with them, but they had no experience with relationships or figuring out how to make them stay.

I gritted my teeth as I knocked on the bakery's rear entrance. When no one responded, I knocked more loudly, and after a moment, the door swung inward and Danny grinned up at me.

"Ev!" he exclaimed. "I couldn't help but notice you were nowhere to be seen last night, and neither was Milo." He arched an eyebrow. "Coincidence?"

"No," I grumbled. There was no point playing coy. Danny would get the truth out of me anyway. "We spent the night together."

He stepped aside. "Come in. Tell me all." He closed the door behind me, then added, "Not all, actually. I don't need the nasty details. I already hear enough about my super hot brothers from literally every other omega in town."

Once, I would have preened at the comment, but now the only omega I wanted to notice me was tucked up in a bed at my parents' place, possibly confused about why he was alone.

"We didn't mate," I said, since that question would no doubt be at the front of his mind. "Or go all the way. But what we did was incredible. I feel so connected with him, and the fact that he trusts me enough to be vulnerable like that after what he's been through blows my mind."

Danny's eyes goggled. "Um, wow." He grabbed a mug of coffee from the counter and drank. "Who are you and what did you do with my stoic brother?"

I shrugged, unselfconscious. I didn't care who knew I was a goner over Milo. "The problem is, he's not a shifter."

Danny's smile vanished abruptly and he slammed his mug down. "If you say one more bigoted—"

"Whoa, whoa." I held up my hands. "Not like that. I'm fine with him being human. He's perfect as he is. But humans don't mate the way we do. They date for years sometimes before getting married. I can't just bite him and be done with it."

"I'm glad you know that," he said sternly. "Consent is important."

I rolled my eyes. "But I can't wait years to claim him either. It's going to make me crazy."

"Hmm." He sounded thoughtful. "I see your problem. Say you were a human and you'd met this guy and really liked him, but didn't know anything about mates. What would you do?"

I squinted at him, thinking hard. The truth was, I'd only ever had hookups, and I couldn't imagine the protocol was the same. "Ask him on a date?"

"Bingo." He made finger guns at me. "Dad will give you the all-clear to tell him about us eventually, but in the meantime, you'll have to court him as though you're human. That means no biting, no knotting, and absolutely no shifting."

"Or sniffing," I murmured.

Danny cocked his head in question.

"Apparently it's weird," I explained.

"Interesting. I'll keep that in mind. No sniffing the humans." He grinned. "This is going to be so much fun to watch."

I groaned and raked a hand through my hair. "Where do I take him? He doesn't seem like an outdoorsy guy."

"Agreed." Danny sipped his coffee again and glanced at the pastries rising on the oven tray. "I need to get busy soon, so let's wrap this up. How about I put together a picnic basket? Picnics are romantic, and you can take him somewhere you can drive to so he doesn't have to hike if that's not his thing."

"Perfect." I ruffled his hair. "Thanks, brother. You're my favorite."

He shook his head in disbelief but looked secretly pleased. It wasn't a lie. I loved all my brothers, but Danny held a special place in my heart. I think that was why it had hit so hard when I realized he'd been in trouble and not confided in me.

"I'll see you later." I nodded to Danny and let myself out, double checking that the door locked behind me.

Next, I headed to work. I went straight to the kitchen and made myself a coffee. Before I could return to the search and rescue headquarters, Zander stopped me in the hall.

"You're here early," I said.

"You are too." He gave me a pointed look. "I heard back from some of my colleagues from further afield about this rogue wolf pack."

"And?" I needed to know what kind of danger Milo was in.

Zander glanced at my coffee. "You know that stuff will rot your insides."

I glanced skyward and silently begged for patience. "Now isn't the time for one of your health rants, Z."

"Suit yourself. Personally, I treat my organs like they matter."

I waited for him to continue, not taking the bait.

"It's bad news," he told me. "That particular pack, the Red Moon Pack, has been linked to the disappearance of several omega shifters, one of whom was later found dead. Their members have also been accused of assault on a number of occasions, but they move on before law enforcement catches up with them. From what I hear, no other shifter groups have been willing to challenge them directly."

My jaw tightened. "Fuck." Like hell would I let those bastards anywhere near Milo. "You spoke to their Alpha, right? How did he come across?"

"Like an arrogant prick." The reply was immediate. "But

that's not uncommon for Alphas, so I didn't read into it. You know any of us can come across that way at times."

"Maybe, but we wouldn't hurt a defenseless omega."

"No, we wouldn't." Zander scowled. "And you'd better believe I'll be asking questions."

"Hopefully we learn something that helps." Although if this Red Moon Pack had gotten away with their behavior for this long, they were probably good at avoiding the consequences of their actions. "We'll have to tread carefully."

"I know." Zander clapped me on the shoulder. "Lucky that's my job and not yours. All I need you to do is exercise a little self-control and not go after them the way I know you're dying to."

"Come on," I growled. "You'd like to kick his ass too."

"Maybe," he acknowledged. "But we have to do this properly."

"Fine." Sometimes, being the least senior alpha in the family sucked, but I knew Zander had a point. "I won't get in the way. For now. If they come at Milo, you'd better bet your ass I'm going to do some damage."

A steely gleam shone in his eye. "Exactly as it should be."

CHAPTER

THIRTEEN

MILO

When I woke up without Everett, my first thought was that he'd decided he didn't want me, but as soon as I sat up, I spotted a handwritten note on the nightstand that had eased my concern. He'd had to go to work early, but he promised to see me later and had signed it off with two X's. That must mean something.

I joined Melinda and Aaron for breakfast, then helped Melinda bake for the children's home. Today she was making bacon and egg pastries and chocolate chip cookies. I offered to do the cookies since I often baked those for myself, but I'd never tried to make pastry from scratch before. Not properly, anyway.

As we were finishing, Danny sauntered in and flashed me a smile.

"Hi," he said. "You're looking better today. Those cuts and scrapes are starting to clear up."

"Thanks." I'd forgotten they were even there, caught up in the excitement of being with Everett. I wondered if Danny and Melinda knew what we'd done last night. Something in Danny's expression made me think he at least had an inkling. I scanned him, noting a light dusting of white powder—flour?—over his shirt. "Where have you been?"

"The bakery." He grabbed a cookie fresh from the oven and bit into it. "Gods, that's good."

I flushed. "Are you a baker?"

"A pastry chef, technically." He polished off the cookie and licked melted chocolate from his fingers. "Nice work."

I looked down at my feet, not sure how to handle getting praised for my baking by a pastry chef. Surely he was just being nice.

"Are you on your break?" Melinda asked, swatting his hand away as he reached for another cookie. "No, those are for the children."

"I am." He grabbed a jar of honey from the cupboard and dunked a spoon into it. "I didn't want Milo to be alone with that, uh, weirdo around, so I thought I'd come over."

"Don't I count?" Melinda sounded indignant. "He's not alone if I'm here."

Danny cringed. "You know what I mean, Momma."

"I hate that I'm putting you both out like this," I said, wondering once again whether it would be best if I just packed my bags and left. I doubted I was in any real danger, regardless of Tomas's supposedly violent history. If he'd wanted to make a move, surely he would have done so already.

"You're not putting us out one bit." Danny licked the spoon and gave me a mischievous smile. "I love honey. It's the best. What's your favorite food?"

I blinked rapidly, not sure what to make of the subject change. "I don't really have a favorite. I love all food."

"But you must have something you like best," he insisted.

I bit my lip. Of course there were some things I liked

more than others, but I was telling the truth that I loved all food. When you'd gone without enough, you learned to celebrate every bite. "Not really. I, um, like fresh produce. Fruit and veggies, or things made with fresh ingredients."

For most of my childhood I'd eaten canned or frozen food. Fresh fruit was one of the few splurges I allowed myself now that I could afford it.

"Any in particular?" he asked.

I shrugged. "Not really. I'll eat anything."

He sighed and shook his head. "Just because you can doesn't mean you should. You deserve good things."

I looked away, pretending that something out the window had caught my attention. It might have been a throwaway comment, but I didn't think so. Danny suspected at least a little of my background, and knowing that made me feel exposed. Time to change the subject.

"Where do you want these cookies?"

CHAPTER

FOURTEEN

MILO

"Are you sure you wouldn't like to come?" Melinda asked as she stacked the containers of food and prepared to go to the children's home.

I hesitated. It should be a straightforward answer, but I found myself wavering. Perhaps it would do me good to see what it was like. Melinda insisted it was nice, and seeing that might help lift some of the malaise that seemed to have settled over me since Danny's comment.

"You really should go," Danny urged. "I need to get back to work and Everett would be a bear if he knew you were here alone."

"Okay." Anxiety squeezed my chest, but I breathed slowly until the sensation eased. He was right. Everett wouldn't want me to be here alone, and I cared about Everett, so I should do what I could to make him happy. Besides, what harm would it do? I'd already survived years in and out of those homes. At worst, it might stir up a few unpleasant memories.

"Great!" He reached for my hand and held it briefly in a

silent show of support. "You'll have fun. The kids are lovely."

I hoped he was right.

"Come along, then." Melinda lifted the containers and carried them out of the kitchen.

"I can help," I said, hurrying after her.

"We only need to get them to the car." She led me out through the front entrance and opened the door of a neat gray sedan parked beside the house. I hadn't noticed it before, but then I'd hardly been out of the house. "We could walk from here, but I prefer to drive when I'm transporting food. No need to make things unnecessarily difficult."

"True." I got into the passenger seat and belted up. She finished packing the back seat and waved to Danny, who was wandering toward the open end of the cul-de-sac.

The drive only lasted a couple of minutes. As Melinda drove along a main street, I spotted a bakery, where I assumed Danny worked, a tattoo parlor, a hairdresser, a supermarket, and several tourist businesses. She turned at a corner with a blocky colonial building that looked like a pub, and stopped in front of a large house the next block over.

I studied the home carefully. If not for the small plaque out front, I might assume it was a normal residential house. The boards had been painted white sometime in the past few years and the yard was well maintained. That was a good start, but it didn't mean the home wasn't one of those with strict managers who ran it like a military camp.

"Let's go." Melinda pushed her door open and gathered the food. I grabbed a container of cookies so at least I'd have something to occupy my hands. We walked up the concrete path to the front door. Melinda knocked and waited. After a moment, the door opened and a golden-haired little girl with a gap-toothed smile beamed out at us.

"Momma Melinda!" she exclaimed, bouncing on the spot. "What do you have today?"

I scanned the girl, doing a quick inventory. She had clean hair in dual braids with pink ribbons at the ends, clear skin, bright eyes, and comfortable—if somewhat outdated—clothes. Her cheeks were plump and she clearly wasn't afraid of Melinda. She looked as well cared for as the yard. I relaxed a fraction. So far, so good.

"I have cookies and pastries," Melinda said. "But you'll have to wait until lunch is served."

The girl pouted. "Okay, Momma." She cocked her head, staring at me curiously. "Who are you?"

I knelt to her height and held out my hand, as if she were an adult. "I'm Milo. What's your name?"

"I'm Lacey." She took my hand and I shook it, amazed by how small it was within my own.

"It's nice to meet you, Lacey."

"Are you a bear?" she asked, her eyes flicking to Melinda in question.

I laughed. I didn't know they taught kids this young about gay slang. "I'm very definitely not a bear. More of a twink, but I'm not quite pretty enough for that."

She looked confused. "Like a Twinkie?"

"Close enough," I decided.

Melinda chuckled. "The kitchen is this way."

I followed her inside, instantly comforted by the fact the interior was as pleasant as the exterior. We passed several bedrooms, where beds were tidily made but the presence of stuffed animals and children's books softened their appearance. A boy a year or two older than Lacey waved shyly from an open living space. In the kitchen, a short male omega in a stylish vest turned from the counter to greet Melinda. His eyes crinkled at the corners and he laid a hand on the back of Lacey's head as she went to his side and slipped her hand into his.

"Good timing," he told Melinda. "We're nearly ready to dish everything up. Susan already came by with the salad." His gaze alighted on me. "Hello. I'm George. Who might you be?"

For the second time in a matter of minutes, I offered a stranger my hand. "I'm Milo. I'm staying with Melinda and Aaron this week."

"Ah, yes." He pursed his lips. "The omega with the unlucky taste in men."

Hopefully not anymore.

I glanced down at my hands, not wanting him nor Melinda to see my expression. I wasn't sure how much Everett wanted others to know about us yet.

"Does everyone know about that?" I asked.

"Don't be embarrassed, honey." He sounded sympathetic. "It's not your fault your date was a creep. And yes, Grizzly Ridge is small, so you should generally assume that everyone knows everything at all times."

"Oh." It seemed so strange to me. Growing up in foster families and group homes in Grayton, I'd always known that if I walked out the door and disappeared, there was a good chance only one or two people would notice I was missing—and even then, they probably wouldn't care enough to do something about it. The idea of an entire community being interlinked was foreign.

"Why don't you two stay for lunch?" George asked.

I started to politely refuse, not wanting to take food out of the mouths of children, but Melinda brushed off my protest.

"Don't worry," she murmured after George had instructed us to gather the children at the table. "There's more than enough."

My face heated. I hated that she'd read my mind. Especially when, as with Danny, it implied she thought she knew something about my background. But then, perhaps I radiated needy orphan vibes.

Melinda knocked on each door along the hall and called for the children to come out to lunch, then she showed me through a doorway into a room dominated by a long, narrow dining table where plates and cutlery were already laid out.

"George sits there," she said, pointing to a space halfway along one side. "He's the center's manager, and he likes to be in the thick of it so the kids know they can approach him. Leave a few spaces on either side." She gestured to a setting near one end. "Here should be good."

I sat, and she took the chair opposite. The little boy I'd seen earlier entered and claimed the seat beside the one Melinda had said was George's. Other children trickled in. A pair of adorable, brown-skinned girls who might have been twins, each with their hair braided and intertwined with colored thread. An older girl, perhaps fourteen or fifteen, corralled the others into their chairs, playing the role of mother hen.

The last to enter, ushered in by George, was a kid of around seventeen with bright blue eyes emphasized by eyeliner, a slender build verging on skinny, and a long skirt wrapped around their slim hips. They scanned the seats, which had mostly been filled, and their gaze fell on the chair beside me, which was still empty. They flashed me a suspicious look and sashayed over, their eyes flicking to me every few seconds, as if wary I might attack. That wariness made me sad, but it was more akin to what I was used to than the apparent happiness of the other children who lived here.

"Hey," they said as they sat, their voice soft and melodious. They smiled at Melinda. "Hi, Momma Melinda."

"Hello, Sam," Melinda said. "This is Milo. He's staying with us."

"I heard." Sam studied me with equal parts interest and caution. "You're from the city?"

"Grayton," I said, which was probably what Sam meant, but I wanted to clarify.

Sam nodded. "I'm thinking about moving there when I finish school."

George cleared his throat. "Let's say grace, shall we?"

I pressed my palms together and bowed my head, more out of habit than any belief in the divine. George shared a few words and invited us to eat.

"Do you like the city?" Sam asked as we reached for the food in the center of the table. Most of the children took their time, unlike the feeding frenzies I'd grown accustomed to when I was younger.

"It's okay. I've never lived anywhere else, so I can't really compare. What do you want to do there?"

Sam shrugged their narrow shoulders. "I'd like to go to a fashion design school, but I won't be able to afford it unless I get a scholarship, so it all relies on my grades."

I sighed in sympathy. "It was the same for me. So stressful at the time, but I'm glad I did it."

They frowned. "You got a scholarship? What did you study?"

"Accounting." I cut into the pie and shoved a large portion into my mouth, chewing and swallowing before I continued. "I grew up in the system too, so it was a struggle to stay afloat but I managed it and I know you will too."

They smiled shyly, some of the wariness dissipating. "Thanks. I hope so." They gave me a once-over. "You don't look much older than me."

"I'm twenty-three, but I get that a lot because I'm short." Perhaps one day I'd be grateful for looking younger than my years, but that day hadn't come yet.

We chatted while we ate, and then I helped with the cleanup. By the time Melinda said it was time to go, I'd promised Sam that they could visit me in Grayton if they ever wanted.

"Wait!" George called as we headed for the door. He raced along the hall and stopped in front of us, breathing heavily. "How long are you in town for?" he asked me.

"Just this week," I replied, wishing for a moment that it could be longer.

"Can you come back before you go?" he asked. "Sam seemed to enjoy your company and it's rare for them to open up to people. It would be good for them to see you again."

"Okay." I liked Sam. "If that's all right with Melinda."

"Of course, Milo." She sounded delighted as she rested a hand on my shoulder. "It will be a pleasure to have company for my trips here."

CHAPTER

FIFTEEN

EVERETT

I stopped at the local florist's on the way home in the evening and picked up a bouquet of red roses for Milo. I didn't want him to have any doubt about my intentions. I parked outside my parents' house and followed my nose to Milo, who was reading one of Momma's novels, his small frame barely spanning the length of the sofa. I paused to take him in. Those eyes, such a unique shade, worked their way across the page, and a furrow formed between his brows as if he were deep in thought.

"Hi," I said.

He shrieked and shot upright, his hand clutching his chest. "Whoa. Everett." He blinked rapidly and set the book down. "Don't scare me like that."

"Sorry, baby." The endearment slipped off my tongue easily. Whether or not he knew it yet, Milo was mine. Mine to hold. Mine to protect. Mine to mate. I offered him the flowers. "Will you come out to dinner with me?"

He blushed, his gaze locked on the flowers as a grin

spread across his face. "These are for me?" His tone was almost reverent.

"Yes." I'd give him roses every damn day if they made him smile like this.

"Thank you." He stood and took them from me slowly, as if he were afraid I might snatch them away. "I've never been given flowers before."

My bear hummed in satisfaction, pleased to be the first, but the human part of my brain wanted Milo to have always been treated well because he deserved it. Were alphas in Grayton stupid? Why had no one spoiled him before?

He raised his eyes to mine, and they glimmered with emotion. "Can we put them in a vase?"

"I'm sure Momma will have one in the kitchen." I nodded toward the door and he preceded me down the hall to the kitchen, where dinner was cooking but Momma was mysteriously absent. She'd probably heard us and wanted to give us space. I searched the cupboards until I found a crystal vase and passed it to Milo. He partially filled it with water and placed it on the kitchen counter, then carefully removed the roses from their wrapping and eased them into the vase. He positioned it at the end of the counter, near the fruit bowl, and beamed.

"They're beautiful," he said. "Thank you so much, Everett."

"Anything for you."

His eyes softened. "By the way, I'd love to go to dinner with you."

Thank Gods. I hadn't overlooked his lack of an answer, but I'd hoped he was distracted by the roses rather than delaying until he figured out how to let me down.

He glanced down at himself. "Will I need to change?"

I took advantage of the opportunity to check him out.

That tight little body. Those lithe legs clad in jeans. "No, you're perfect."

His blush deepened and he looked down at his feet.

"Let's go." I took his hand and led him out to my car. I opened the passenger-side door for him and closed it before circling around.

"Where are we going?" Milo asked as I started the engine and pulled onto the road.

"There's a lovely spot I'd like to show you," I told him. "It's near the stream. Is that okay?" I needed to keep in mind that he'd already had one bad date with an alpha so far this week. He might be nervous to be alone with me.

"Sounds nice."

He seemed fascinated by the scenery as we entered town, keeping his attention fixed firmly outside the window. I supposed he hadn't had the chance to look around yet. All the more for me to show him. When I stopped outside the bakery, Danny was already standing outside, holding a large cane picnic basket. I opened the window and he passed it inside.

"Have fun." He gave an exaggerated wink.

"Thanks, Dan."

He rolled his eyes. "I suppose I meant you, too."

He backed away, chuckling, and I closed the window again and handed the basket to Milo.

His breath caught. "We're having a picnic?"

"Yeah. I hope you like them and that it's not too cheesy."

"I've never been on one before." He gripped the basket tightly, and I couldn't resist leaning over to kiss his cheek. "I'm excited for my first picnic."

"Hopefully you'll enjoy it."

He smiled at me shyly. "I'm sure I will."

I waved to Danny and pulled away from the curb. It

took five minutes to arrive at the clearing outside of town beside a small, babbling stream. When we got out, I discovered the grass was soft but damp, so I folded a blanket from the back of the car for us to sit on. Milo placed the basket in the center of the blanket, handling it as though it were fragile. He was breaking my heart with how awed he seemed by the simplest of things, but I was glad I was the one who got to introduce him to them.

I sat on one side of the blanket and opened the basket, leaning over to see what was inside. There were sandwiches, a couple of pastries, and a large tub of fresh fruit salad.

Milo cried out in delight and reached for the fruit salad. "Is this why Danny was asking me about my favorite food earlier?" he asked.

"It is." I'd been surprised when Danny had told me of his preference for fresh fruit and vegetables but when I thought about it, it made sense. He probably hadn't had much of them growing up. "Do you like it?"

He gazed at me with shining eyes. "It's perfect. Thank you."

He served fruit salad onto a paper plate also within the basket and dug in. He ate like a starving man, and I watched for a few seconds before I realized I was being rude. He licked his lips, and I had to look away, willing my dick not to get overexcited.

Be a good bear, I reminded myself. *Take it slow.*

Milo shivered.

I frowned. "Are you cold?"

His sweater looked warm, but he probably wasn't used to being in the outdoors like this.

"A little," he admitted.

"Here." I shrugged off my coat and offered it to him.

His eyes widened. "I couldn't. What about you?"

"I run hot." All shifters did. Not that I could explain that.

"Are you sure?" He looked hesitant.

"Yes. Put it on." He took the coat from me and wrapped it around himself. It swamped him.

He buried his nose in the fabric and inhaled deeply. "Mm. It smells like you."

Oh fuck. I bit my lower lip hard to hold in a groan. Damn, that was sexy. I wanted to cover him in my scent and never let him wash it off.

While we ate, we chatted about the sort of stuff I imagined was common on a first date. Our jobs, our families, our likes and dislikes. I learned that Milo enjoyed baking but really loved cooking, and that being an accountant didn't thrill him but he craved the financial security that came with it. We veered away from deeper topics. I didn't ask about his childhood because I wanted to keep the mood light. That could come later. He seemed fascinated by the fact I had a tight-knit family who all lived within a few hundred yards of each other. I caught a hint of wistfulness in his expression and wanted to promise that they could be his family too, but I didn't want to get too intense and scare him.

"It's time to head back," I said eventually, after the sun had long since ducked beneath the horizon and the night was steadily growing darker.

Milo sighed. "It feels like we only just got here."

"I know." I took his hand and squeezed it. "I had a great time."

"Me too." That gorgeous smile of his reappeared. He was still hesitant—I got the impression he was holding back a lot of his thoughts and feelings—but he was beginning to trust me, and I'd do anything to protect that fragile trust. "This was the best first date I've ever had."

"Mine, too." I kissed his palm, rubbing my face against it, wishing I could shift and have him stroke me all over. "Let's get you home, sweet boy."

We drove back in companionable silence. I could swear the finest thread of a connection was beginning to form between us, even without the mating bond. I felt warm and content, and I didn't think it was only my own emotions I was basking in. When I parked outside my parents' house, I got out and hurried around to open the door for him before he could do it himself, hiding a smile when he indulged me without any fuss. My beautiful omega deserved everything, and I wanted to give it to him.

"I'll walk you to the door," I said.

"Wait."

I glanced down at him just in time to see his tongue dart out and moisten his lips. "What is it, baby?"

He hesitated. "Can I have a kiss first?"

I melted. "Of course."

With one hand I cradled his face, and I used the other to guide him back against the side of my car. He stretched onto his toes and kissed me gently. I pressed him against the car with my body, my thigh sliding between his legs. Milo gasped and tentatively licked into my mouth. I opened, letting him take the lead. The kiss turned fiery as he rocked against my thigh. I could feel his stiff cock through his jeans. He whimpered, and I swallowed it.

"Ev," he panted. "I've never felt like this."

"Like what?" I murmured, trailing kisses down the side of his neck and burying my face in the crook of his shoulder, practically aching to bite him.

"Like I'm hungry for you. I need you so much." He sounded desperate and confused. Poor baby. I'd grown up understanding the concept of mates but this was all new for him.

"Take what you need. I've got you."

He rode my thigh, rubbing himself shamelessly against me. My own cock throbbed and leaked, especially when the scent of his slick hit my nostrils. My perfect omega was ready for me, his body preparing to take me in even though he'd never taken a man before. I wanted to thrust into him, but if I did, I'd mate with him. At the moment, I didn't even trust myself to come without claiming him.

"You're so hot." His head fell back and he worked his hips harder, getting himself off on my leg. A rush of pride slammed through me as he keened with pleasure and the salty sharp aroma of come filled my nostrils.

He sagged. I kissed him softly, using all of my restraint not to take him. My bear didn't understand why we couldn't just bite him. Mark him. Make him ours. I had to get out of there before he pushed to the surface and took what he wanted.

"You're beautiful." I kissed his forehead and backed off, adjusting the coat to hide any wetness on his jeans. Not that it would stop my parents from smelling him the moment he entered the house, but he didn't know about their enhanced senses and I wanted to preserve whatever of his dignity I could. "Go inside now."

"But what about you?" He pouted, and the expression was so uncharacteristic I had to chuckle.

"I'm fine. Go."

He harrumphed. "Fine. Be like that."

He strode past me and up the steps to the door, glancing back over his shoulder to blow me a kiss so I knew he wasn't really upset. I waited until the door latched behind him and raced home to take care of myself.

SIXTEEN

MILO

I was baking with Melinda the next day when there was a knock on the door. Melinda called for whoever it was to come through to the kitchen. A couple in their late thirties strode in a moment later, smiling warmly.

"We're here to see the clan Alpha," the man announced.

I frowned. What was a clan Alpha? Melinda glanced at me and then gave the man a meaningful look.

"Um, I mean Aaron." The guy seemed flustered. "We need to discuss something with him."

My frown deepened in confusion at his unusual phrasing. Did that mean Aaron was "the clan Alpha"? Was that some kind of job title? I'd been under the impression he was a doctor or something, although I didn't know what had made me think that.

"It's about the run," the man added, glancing at me again in a way that made me uncomfortable. "The night run, you know."

Yeah, he was definitely trying to speak in code, and I

didn't like it. It made me feel as though they were keeping secrets from me. Unease prickled up my back.

"Excuse me," I said to Melinda. "I've got a bit of a headache. I might go and lie down if that's okay."

"Of course, Milo." A look of relief flickered across her features. Something was definitely up. "Let me know if you need an aspirin."

"I will." I retreated to the bedroom and locked the door for the first time. I needed space to think. It was possible I was overreacting, but I definitely had the feeling that Melinda didn't want me to know what the couple were talking about. Was it because they'd said something about "the clan Alpha"—whatever that was? Perhaps it was a rank in some kind of organization. My stomach dropped. A gang, maybe. As for the run... what was that? A literal run? At night? Wouldn't that be a death wish around here? Perhaps they meant a supply run, but a supply of what? Food? Drugs? Weapons?

No, that would be crazy, right? Aaron and his family had been nice to me. Surely he wasn't involved in organized crime. But then what? I shuddered, my imagination running crazy. I had no evidence that they even were who they said they were, or that I'd gotten here the way they'd described. Only their word for it. For all I knew, they could be keeping me here under false pretenses.

You sound insane.

Even though I knew my thoughts were unhinged, I couldn't dismiss them. Something wasn't right, and drugs seemed like the simplest explanation. I stared out the window, wondering if I ought to climb out and hitch a ride back to Grayton. But if dangerous things were happening in this town, getting into a car with a stranger might be equivalent to leaping out of the frying pan and into the fire.

How do I get out of here?

My panic grew. I was trapped. Sure, everyone here seemed nice, but appearances could be deceiving. I'd experienced plenty of that during my years in foster care and group homes. My thoughts ventured to Everett. Big, gruff Everett who treated me like I was precious. He couldn't be involved in anything illegal, could he? It was crazy. He couldn't fake the way he looked at me. It was real. I meant something to him.

Or maybe you're just his new toy.

My heart sank. Yeah, that could be it. I was the bright, shiny omega he got to play with until they decided to kill me and hide my body in the woods.

Someone knocked on the door and my heart rammed against my ribs. I clutched my chest, trying to contain my fear. I'd survived shitty situations before, and I could get through this. The handle turned, but the door didn't open. Thank the Gods for locks.

"Hey, Milo." It was Danny, and he sounded confused. "Are you in there? Momma said you have a headache."

Shit. Should I open the door? Or were they out there, waiting for that, so they could attack me? I shook my head. I was being ridiculous. I drew in a deep breath, tiptoed across the room, and unclicked the lock. The door opened slowly and Danny's concerned face came into view.

"Are you okay?" Danny asked. "You're really pale."

"I'm fine. Just a headache." I didn't move from the doorway. I wouldn't invite him into the room.

"You really don't look so good." He tried to guide me backward, toward the bed, but I resisted. He arched an eyebrow. "Momma said it came on suddenly, just as we had visitors."

"Mm-hmm," I mumbled noncommittally.

He squinted at me, scanning my features, his mouth

twisted in thought. "Is it really a headache or did something happen?"

My pulse racing, I surreptitiously wiped my sweaty palms on my shirt. So that was it. They'd sent Danny to find out how much I knew or suspected.

"N-Nothing happened," I stammered. "Honestly. I think I'm tired. Maybe it's the shock of the weekend finally hitting me."

"Maybe." He sounded dubious. "Or maybe you're stressed about something else and it's making you unwell."

My shoulders slumped. He wasn't going to let this go. "I don't know what's going on here, but you're all hiding something. If you're going to kill me, just do it already, or let me go."

"What?" Danny's eyes widened. "Why would you think we want to kill you?"

I shrugged. "Drugs. Gang stuff. I don't know."

He barked out a sharp laugh. "We're not into drugs or gang activities, I promise."

"Then what?" I demanded.

He hesitated. "I can't tell you."

I pursed my lips. Of course not. "I'd like to go, please."

He frowned. "Go where?"

"Away from here." I'd have thought that was obvious. "If you're not keeping me against my will, then I want to leave." I started toward the door, determination replacing the fear that had been stewing inside me.

"No!" He flung up his hands to stop me. "Please don't leave. Everett will be devastated."

I gave him a look that told him to cut the crap, but he shook his head.

"I mean it," he said. "Everett cares about you, and I swear to the Gods, no one here means you harm." He moistened his lips and glanced at the door, then back to me. "I can't explain, but I'll talk to Dad and hopefully he can clear everything up. Please, just stay one more night. If you still want to leave tomorrow, nobody will stop you."

I didn't know why, but I believed him. Maybe it made me a fool, but despite my lingering anxiety, I'd heard the truth in his voice when he'd said no one meant me harm.

"One more night," I said. After all, I could always escape under the cover of darkness if I had to. Even if it meant walking all the way back to Grayton. I was strong. I'd endured worse.

SEVENTEEN

MILO

After our conversation, Danny persuaded me to go to the bakery with him for a treat. We walked over together, intentionally keeping the conversation light. He told me how he'd always wanted to be a baker, and that he'd been lucky enough to be able to do it without leaving Grizzly Ridge. I was still on edge, but I shared a couple of stories about nightmare clients. Anyone who says accountants don't have good work stories is lying. Do you know how many illicit activities can be uncovered just by seeing a credit card charge in the wrong place?

When we got to the bakery, Danny led me to the display cabinet. "You like fruit, right?"

"Yes."

He pointed to a fruit pastry. "You should try this." He pointed at a donut dusted with cinnamon sugar. "Or this. It has apples in the center, cooked with apple spice and brown sugar."

"Yum. I'll take one of each, please." Why not? He was offering and it wasn't often I treated myself.

"Great choice." Danny went behind the counter and

placed one of each in a paper bag, then passed them over to me. "Enjoy. And seriously, you don't have to worry about your safety here. I promise."

I flushed, embarrassed at the thought that one of the other customers might overhear his comment. No doubt I sounded paranoid. "Okay."

I didn't tell him I believed him. I might be inclined to, but the voice of doubt wouldn't disappear.

"I'll see you later?" he prompted. I knew it was his way of asking if I'd keep my word about staying.

"You will."

"Good." He flashed his teeth. "For the record, Everett loves anything with caramel or honey, if you ever want to surprise him."

"Thanks." I beelined for the exit before he could notice my blush. As I stepped outside, it occurred to me that I'd be making the walk back on my own when I wasn't supposed to be going anywhere without protection. But it was a short walk and there was no proof I was in danger, so I decided to chance it. I'd just go fast.

I hurried across the road and down the sidewalk. I rounded a corner and spotted a white van parked on the roadside. A male omega stood at the front, looking under the hood. The engine seemed to be steaming. I hesitated, torn between whether to ignore him or ask if everything was okay. Politeness won out.

"Having engine trouble?" I asked.

"Yeah." He glanced up, his expression wry. "Could you come and have a look? I've got no idea what any of this stuff is."

"I doubt I'll be any help. I know less than nothing about engines." But I moved a little closer, peering over in case anything was obviously wrong.

A pair of hands grabbed me from the side and lifted me

off my feet. I shouted in surprise, dropping the bags from the bakery as I struggled to free myself. The omega met my eyes and mouthed, "I'm sorry," and then something covered my head. I heard the door slide open and I was dumped in the back, my hip and shoulder hitting the hard floor. I screamed as loudly as I could through the fabric over my face, but it wasn't enough.

Then a roar filled my ears. It was animalistic and wrathful. I shivered, certain that whatever it was, it was coming for me. But instead, I heard a scuffle behind me. Men grunted and cursed. It fell silent. A moment later, I was lifted gently out of the vehicle and the covering was removed from my head. Everett's face came into view, his eyes shining gold as they searched me for injuries. With a sob of relief, I wrapped myself around him and clung.

"Please don't let me go."

"Never, baby," he promised. "Never fucking again."

EIGHTEEN

EVERETT

I wanted to spill blood. Some asshole had thought it was acceptable to kidnap my omega in my town in the middle of the day, and they needed to suffer the consequences. I wouldn't tolerate anyone scaring Milo, no matter who or what they were. If it weren't for the fact I'd been nearby and scented his distress, I might not have been here in time to save him.

I clutched Milo to my chest and inhaled his warm, fruity scent. I never wanted to let him go. If I could strap him to my back and take him everywhere with me, I would. And yes, I knew that sounded insane, but he made me lose my mind.

He's all right, I reminded myself. *He's safe.*

My fangs started to drop and I closed my eyes and focused on shifting my teeth back to normal. When I opened my eyes again, Milo drew away and frowned up at me.

"Your eyes look strange," he said.

I blinked, trying to mask them. "Do they?"

His frown deepened. "They did," he said. "But now they don't. Maybe I imagined it."

My chest tightened. I hated the fact I had to mislead him. I wished I could just tell him the truth, but there was no saying how he'd react, and the Alpha would be furious with me if I shared our secret without permission.

"Let's get back to the police station," Zander said. He'd been with me when I'd gotten the silent S.O.S. from Milo, and he'd followed in his cruiser in case I needed help. Now, I could see that he'd secured both the alpha and the omega kidnappers with handcuffs. The alpha was already in the cruiser while the omega stammered apologies and terrified explanations. I wasn't in the mood to listen.

"Okay. I need to hear what these assholes want with Milo." I swept Milo into my arms, ignoring his protest. "Let me carry you, baby," I murmured. "I need you close."

He stopped resisting and rested his head against my pec. "Okay."

"Can you walk over with this one?" Zander asked, gesturing to the omega kidnapper. "Can I trust you to return him in one piece?"

I glared at the squirmy little man. "I won't hurt him unless he tries to run."

I lifted the bottom of my jacket so he could see the gun on my hip.

He paled. "I won't try anything."

"You'd better not." While gunshot wounds weren't always lethal to shifters, they were more dangerous to omegas, who healed slower than alphas, and they fucking hurt.

Zander nodded and got into his cruiser. "See you there."

As we started walking, the omega tried to apologize again, but I shut him up with a growl. He stayed silent after that, and

I was relieved when we arrived at the station and one of the officers escorted him into an interview room. While I wanted to hear what was going on, I'd liked to be able to focus on Milo, and the omega had messed with my ability to do that.

"Are you okay?" I asked softly, brushing the hair back from his forehead.

"I think so." His voice was strained. "But I don't understand what those guys want with me."

"Neither do I." It bothered me. If the culprit had been Tomas, I would have understood. As it was, my best guess was that the alpha was one of his pack mates. The omega smelled like bobcat, not wolf, so I wasn't sure how he fit in. Perhaps he was one of the omegas who'd been taken by the rogue pack and was being held against his will—or he had a major case of Stockholm syndrome. Whatever the case, he was as guilty as the alpha as far as I was concerned because he'd been used to lull Milo into a false sense of security.

Zander exited one of the interview rooms and locked it behind himself. "Milo, do you feel up to talking me through what happened before I question them?"

"He needs time," I grumped, but to my surprise, Milo shushed me.

"I can do it now," he said. "Better to get it out of the way." He hesitated. "Do we have to go into one of those rooms?"

"No." Zander produced a voice recorder from his pocket. "You tell me what happened and I'll record it on this. One of the administrators will type it up and we'll get you to sign the statement."

I tipped my head to Zander, acknowledging that he was doing his best to minimize the number of times Milo would have to relive the attack.

"Where do you want me to start?" Milo asked.

"Start when you left the bakery and go from there," Zander told him.

Milo paused to gather his thoughts and then falteringly walked us through every detail of his journey from the bakery to the back of the white van. When he finished, Zander smiled kindly and thanked him.

"Would you like to listen to the interviews with the perps?" he asked.

Milo's eyes widened. "We can do that?"

Zander chuckled. "Not technically, no, so be sure not to tell on me."

"We won't." Milo's promise was so damn earnest I couldn't resist the urge to kiss his forehead and snuggle him close.

"I'd like to hear what they have to say for themselves," I told Zander.

"You can watch from the observation room."

"Thanks."

I rose, keeping Milo firmly in my arms, and carried him to the doorway between the entrances to the two interview rooms. Inside, a desk occupied the center of the room with several chairs around it. Windows stretched the length of each side wall, showing the alpha kidnapper in one adjoining room and the omega in the other.

Zander started with the alpha. "Why did you attempt to kidnap Milo Silva?"

The alpha shrugged like he didn't have a care in the world. Asshole. "Tomas said his mate had gone off half-cocked and needed to be collected and brought home."

My teeth ground together. Milo was *not* Tomas's mate.

"Mate?" Milo asked quietly. I pretended not to hear.

"Tomas claimed that Mr. Silva is his partner?" Zander asked, neatly rephrasing so I wouldn't have to.

The alpha looked at Zander as if he were thick. "Not just his partner. His fated."

I stood. I wanted to hear everything, but if we stayed in here any longer, Milo might find out about shifters despite my best efforts.

"Where are we going?" he asked. "I wanted to hear the rest."

"Later," I said. "Zander will have a recording." He could listen until his heart was content after he'd learned the truth from me. "For now, I want to get you home and hold you."

NINETEEN

MILO

I woke with Everett wrapped around me, the air filled with his masculine scent, his heart beating powerfully beneath my cheek. I was as close to him as I could get, and it didn't feel like enough. I wanted to become one with him in a way I didn't understand.

I looked around for a clock but didn't see one. The curtains were drawn, but it wasn't completely dark outside. It could have been evening or early morning, but something told me it was evening. Everett's phone was on the nightstand so I grabbed it and checked. Seven o'clock. We'd slept for a couple of hours.

I slowly disentangled myself from him and scanned his body, appreciating the view. His arms were muscled and tattooed. His chest was broad and perfect to rest on. His face was relaxed in sleep, the determined set of his chin absent and his usual intensity dialed down. His hands...

My jaw dropped. His hands were battered, the knuckles flecked with blood and anointed with shades of yellow and green that confused me because it looked like older bruising than it actually was. I snatched one up, desperate to make sure he was okay, and gently tested his palm and fingers. Despite the damage, they all seemed intact. I'd become good at identifying broken fingers over the course of my childhood. A couple of my own were slightly bent from healing without proper medical attention. Everett must have injured himself when he'd been rescuing me. I hated the thought.

I stretched out my limbs, checking each one for pain. My elbows and knees were sore from having been tossed in the back of the van, and my head ached—probably from a combination of the adrenaline come-down and a good old-fashioned whack. One of my hips was tender. It must have taken the brunt of the landing. Everywhere else seemed in reasonably good condition. Thank Gods.

I settled against Everett again and closed my eyes, but immediately the sight of the omega's face filled my mind as he mouthed "I'm sorry." I grimaced. Why had he and that alpha tried to take me? From what little I recalled of the alpha's interview, I had the impression they were friends of Tomas. But if that was the case, then why hadn't Tomas been there himself?

Maybe he had.

A sick feeling washed over me.

Perhaps Tomas had been watching and waiting for his moment, but Everett and Zander's arrival had scared him off. I bit my tongue so I wouldn't whimper. I just didn't understand why Tomas was apparently fixated on me. We'd talked for fifteen minutes, and he'd kept up a mono-logue most of that time. The obsession wasn't rational. Or sane.

Why can't he just leave me alone?

Tears prickled my eyes. Was there some karmic sign on my back saying "kick me"? Surely other people didn't have problems like this.

"Shh, baby." Everett's arms tightened around me. "What's wrong?"

I blinked rapidly, trying to hold back the rising tide of emotion threatening to take me under. "Nothing."

He stroked the back of my head and placed one of his massive hands on my lower back. A tear leaked out of one eye. I felt so safe with him around me. Safer than I ever had before. But I didn't know if I could trust it after the strangeness of the past few days.

"You can tell me," he said. "I'm here for you."

Another tear trickled down my face and dripped onto his chest. "I just feel like everything is completely crazy and I have no control over anything and no idea what's going on."

Everett's chest expanded as he inhaled. "I wish I could fix it for you."

"I'll be okay." Milo sniffled. "I'm stronger than I look."

"I'm sure you are, but you don't always have to be. You can let go with me. Let it out."

Letting go sounded really good. I was so tired of holding everything together all the time. I stopped holding back and gave in to the tears. Everett held me close and I buried my face in his chest. Despite my confusion, I felt safer with his arms around me than I could ever remember feeling before.

TWENTY

EVERETT

I hated seeing Milo cry, but it was obvious he'd been keeping too much locked inside for too long and something had to give. I held him and murmured reassurances until he finally ran out of tears.

"How do you feel?" I asked, kissing the top of his head and inhaling a lungful of his delicious scent.

"A little better." His voice was raspy, no doubt thanks to the crying. "I'm confused, Ev. Why did those guys want to kidnap me? They said Tomas called me his mate. What does that mean?"

Shit. I'd hoped he'd forgotten all that. To be honest, I'd half-expected him to pass out from exhaustion so I'd have a reprieve from figuring out how to explain things until the morning.

"And what about the couple who came over earlier?" he demanded.

I frowned. "What couple?"

"I don't know!" Milo exclaimed, clambering off my lap, obviously agitated. "They turned up while we were baking and said they needed to talk to the clan Alpha. What the hell is a clan Alpha? Danny told me it wasn't a criminal thing, but I don't know what to think."

I sighed and reached for his hand, gutted when he pulled it away.

"Please, Ev," he begged. "Tell me. It's making me feel crazy."

I closed my eyes and sucked in a breath. This couldn't wait any longer. "Come for dinner with my family and I'll explain everything."

After I'd checked with Dad. Surely after he heard what Milo had picked up on, he'd know we couldn't delay.

Milo searched my eyes, and he must have found what he was looking for because he nodded. "Okay."

"Thank you." This time, when I reached for his hand, he let me take it. "I'll just call Momma to set it up."

I made the phone call, relieved to hear that she'd already intended to call a family dinner, and that the meal would be ready in half an hour. I relayed the news to Milo.

"Do you mind if I shower?" he asked. "And maybe borrow a set of your clothes?"

"You shower and I'll find you something to change into," I told him. Having a task would keep my mind off his naked body for at least a few minutes. It would be difficult to resist joining him, but it wouldn't feel right to instigate anything sexual while he was in this state.

He smiled, and it warmed my heart. Maybe I wouldn't lose him when he learned the truth. "Thanks."

He scrambled off the bed and headed for the bathroom while I dug around in my closet until I found one of my old high school shirts that, while too big for Milo, would fit him better than anything else would. I paired it with a set of sweatpants Danny had left behind. I rubbed myself all over the pants like the possessive bastard I was so they'd smell like me instead of Danny, then placed them outside the bathroom door.

I waited for Milo in the living room, and when he waltzed in wearing my shirt and smelling of soap and my scent, I wanted to beat my chest. Damn, he was sexy.

"You ready to go?" I asked, offering my hand.

To my delight, he intertwined his fingers with mine. "I'm nervous," he said. "Do I need to be?"

"No." His hand was delicate in mine, and I knew I'd fight for him with everything I had if he were ever in danger again. "You have nothing to fear from my family. I hope you know I'd never put you at risk."

He glanced up and me and moistened his lips. "I'd like to believe that, but I've learned to pay attention to people's actions, not their pretty words."

His statement felt like a needle piercing my heart, but I knew he didn't intend to wound me. He'd been through a lot, and being cautious had kept him alive. "I get it."

I locked the door behind us as we left, sad that I felt the need to when I never had before. I should have known that even Grizzly Ridge couldn't remain completely safe forever. The front door was ajar at my parents' place, so we let ourselves in and followed voices to the dining room, where they were organizing several steaming dishes in the center of the table and Danny was arranging cutlery. When he saw us, he flew toward us and wrapped Milo in a hug.

"I'm so sorry," he wailed. "I should never have made you walk back on your own. If I'd been with you, you never would have been in danger."

Milo was clearly startled by the outburst, but he tentatively hugged Danny and patted his back. "It's okay. I could have refused or asked someone else to come along. Or even waited at the bakery until you could walk me home again."

"But you shouldn't have had to," Danny protested. "I

shouldn't have put you at risk like that. It was thoughtless and I'm sorry a million times over."

Milo patted his back once more and pulled away from him. "There's no way to know whether you being with me would have made a difference. They might have hurt you to get to me and I couldn't live with that."

Danny's eyes flashed to his bear and I gave him a warning look. He blinked, and they returned to normal. I knew what he was thinking. It was unlikely the alpha would have tried to attack them both when he'd have been able to smell what Danny was. Even an omega grizzly could do a lot of damage. But Milo didn't know our secret, and it would have to stay that way until I'd spoken to Dad. Hopefully I'd get the chance to do that tonight so I could confess everything to Milo as I'd promised. If I didn't, I suspected there was every chance he would try to sneak out in the middle of the night—especially if he'd seen Danny's eyes. He was starting to realize that all the strange little things he was noticing added up to something massive.

"We'll have to agree to disagree," Danny said, just as Garrick entered carrying a roasting dish laden with honey-glazed ham.

Milo sniffed appreciatively. "Mm, that smells good."

Momma smiled. "Thank you, darling."

"I think he meant me," Garrick joked, and I had to rein in the impulse to charge at him. I knew he was only teasing, but until I was securely mated to Milo, every teasing remark felt like a threat to our bond and my bear didn't like it.

"Zander is on his way," Melinda said. "Let's sit."

I pulled out a chair for Milo, and when he sat, I took the one beside him. Danny took the seat opposite Milo, with Garrick to his right, and Momma and Dad took the head of the table. Danny filled everyone's glasses with water. I drank from mine gratefully. I hadn't realized how thirsty I was.

When Zander arrived, his grim expression told me all I needed to know about how much useful information he'd gotten out of the kidnappers. I raised an eyebrow and he subtly shook his head. Zander sat, Momma said grace, and we started eating. Milo seemed on edge during the meal, but nothing I said or did relaxed him. Fortunately, my family steered well away from problematic topics like the kidnapping, Tomas, and rogue wolf packs, instead opting to discuss the children's home, the weather, and work. I could tell Milo had noticed the avoidance and that he was suspicious of it, but fortunately, after we retired to the living room, he started dozing. I took advantage of the opportunity to ease myself away from him and gestured for Dad to join me in the other room.

TWENTY-ONE

MILO

I couldn't believe I'd fallen asleep. I'd been on the verge of uncovering whatever secret Everett and his family were keeping, but my body had betrayed me. I felt better now, with a good night of sleep under my belt, but that was beside the point. Even if he'd had to wake me, Everett should have done it. I wanted to know the truth. I *needed* to.

I'd hoped we could have the conversation as soon as I'd awoken, but instead he'd insisted on making me breakfast, and then getting me into the shower. He hadn't even tried to join me, and was now sitting in the hall outside the bathroom. I couldn't help wondering if he was protecting me, or keeping me here. When I got out of the shower, I dried myself and sauntered past him in the nude. I'd intended to make a point, but based on the way his jaw dropped and he ran after me, I didn't think he'd gotten it.

"You're so sexy," he said, stalking toward me across the bedroom. "Are you trying to seduce me?"

"No," I snapped, more testily than I'd meant to. "I'm trying to get your attention."

He winked. "You've got it."

I huffed. "Ev, I get that you're worried about me, but you don't have to babysit me twenty-four-seven. I'm a grown man. I survived some pretty shitty situations growing up and I don't need you to coddle me."

He sighed and rubbed his temples, as though I was being the difficult one. "I hate that you went through that, and I want to hear more about it later, but right now you need to realize that you don't have to be alone anymore. There are people who care for you and want you to be safe."

My squishy heart flopped around like a landed fish. Damn, how was I supposed to hold onto my frustration when he went and said sweet stuff like that? I'd always been alone. There had never been anyone else to rely on, and the idea of letting go tempted me like crazy. But the thing was, I couldn't allow myself to fully lower my guard until I knew what they were hiding.

"It might be easier to accept that if I knew what you're all keeping from me," I said. "I know there's something, so don't try to convince me there isn't."

"I wouldn't do that," Everett said. "I promise I'll tell you. Just let me call Zander and see whether there have been any sightings of Tomas or other strangers in the area first. I need to know whether to be on guard."

"Okay." That seemed reasonable. "But if you slip away without answering me, I'm leaving. I mean it."

"I won't."

His promise should reassure me, but his expression—a mixture of resignation and dread—made me wonder if perhaps I was better off not knowing whatever their secret was.

TWENTY-TWO

EVERETT

I had to come clean, but damn, I didn't want to. There was no way to know how Milo would react. He might run away. But if I didn't say anything, he'd *definitely* run away, so I had no choice but to tell him and hope for the best. First, though, I scraped out a brief reprieve by checking in with Zander. I stayed in the same room as Milo so he'd know I wasn't going to abandon him but kept the phone off speaker in case Zander said something not meant for other ears.

"Hey, brother," Zander said.

"Any sight of them today?" I asked, knowing he'd understand who I was referring to.

"No." He sounded perturbed. "It's quiet. A bit eerie, actually."

"Is the alpha from yesterday still in holding?"

"Of course. He attempted to kidnap someone. He's been arrested and won't be causing any more trouble for your mate."

"Good." I was glad Milo had human hearing, or he'd

have no doubt picked up on Zander's use of the word "mate." "What about the omega?"

Zander sighed. "It seems the poor kid was forced into being an accomplice against his will. The pack *claimed* him —his description, not mine—when they passed through his hometown in Montana. Apparently the alphas use some of the kidnapped omegas for fun and discard them, but keep the ones they think might be useful workhorses. Nicholas—that's the omega—is a chef, so they took him with them to prepare their meals. He was willing to talk to me once he understood that I wouldn't return him to the pack against his will. He's already called his Alpha from home and they're sending someone to come and get him. He's asked me to pass on an apology to Milo."

"Hmm. I'll make sure he hears it. Thanks, Z."

"No problem. Go take care of your mate."

I said goodbye and ended the call.

"What's going on?" Milo asked, his eyes wide and eager. "Have they caught Tomas?"

"No," I admitted, wincing as he visibly deflated. "But one good thing has come from this. Apparently the omega who was involved in your kidnapping attempt—his name is Nicholas—was being coerced into it against his will. With the alpha behind bars, he's free now." I studied Milo's face, trying to gauge how he felt about considering Nicholas as a victim rather than an attacker.

"That must have been awful for him," Milo said. "No wonder he mouthed 'I'm sorry' right before the alpha grabbed me. He might have gone through the exact same thing."

I shook my head. I hadn't even considered that, but he was right. How sick was it to force a prisoner to assist in the capture of another potential prisoner?

"He said he wanted me to pass on an apology."

"I'm sorry for him too," Milo replied. "But don't think you can distract me with that stuff. You still owe me the truth."

I sighed. "You'll get it. Put some clothes on. We're going outside."

"Outside?" His brow furrowed. "Why?"

"Because some things are easier to show than explain."

He dressed in a combination of my and Danny's clothes and followed me outside. My heart was heavy as I locked the door and led him into the woods.

"Where are we going?" he asked. "You're not going to kill me and dispose of my body, are you?"

He was joking, but I could hear the hint of a tremor in his voice and smell the sour tang of his fear. I wanted to bundle him up and comfort him, but he wouldn't thank me for delaying once again, even if it made both of us feel better. Gods, why had I never realized how much of an emotional rollercoaster having a mate would be? I'd always assumed it would be soothing and pleasant. This fierce desire and protectiveness was anything but.

"You're safe with me," I vowed.

Once we'd gone far enough that I doubted anyone would stumble across us, I stopped in a small clearing and turned to him.

"Stay there."

I moved to the other side of the clearing and began removing my clothes.

Milo took a few steps back, his expression switching from surprise to horror to defeat in the blink of an eye. His trembling lower lip made me wonder if he was expecting me to assault him. I tried not to take it personally. I just wished he trusted me.

"Remember what I said. You're safe. I won't hurt you. I just need to take off my clothes to show you something."

Milo's lip curled, but he didn't run. "It's not the first time I've heard that."

My bear roared. He wanted to rip apart anyone who'd tried to get naked with Milo, consensual or not.

I drew in a deep breath to steady my nerves. "My family are bear shifters. Grizzlies, specifically. That means we can alternate between appearing as a human and a bear."

Milo stared at me. I held his gaze. One of his eyes twitched. Then he burst out laughing.

"I get it now," he gasped through spasms of laughter. "You're all insane. That's the big secret. You're completely nuts."

Well, I guessed I'd have to prove it the old-fashioned way if I wanted him to take me seriously. I focused on allowing my body to change and expand, my grizzly coming to the surface. Fur sprouted, bones reformed, and then I stood before him as a beast, waiting to see how he'd respond.

TWENTY-THREE

MILO

Holy fucking fuck, Everett was a bear. He was actually a bear. A massive, shaggy brown bear. A fucking grizzly.

I stumbled backward, tripping over a root, and landed on my ass. The bear started to move toward me but I threw my hands up to shield myself and he stopped.

I couldn't take my eyes off him. It had to be a trick. This couldn't be real. Maybe I'd seen the bear eat Everett, but my mind had been too freaked out by the sight so it had wiped it from my memory. I'd heard of things like that happening.

"S-Stay there." I got to my feet and backed away a few more steps until I was leaning against a large tree. If I had to, I could put the tree between us and it might offer a degree of protection.

The bear moved forward again, but he didn't charge. Instead, he lay on his belly in the center of the clearing, his chin resting on the ground. I frowned. It was a submissive position.

"Everett?" I asked.

The bear raised his head and lowered it, as if he were nodding.

"Holy fuck," I muttered to myself. "You're a bear."

Then I looked closer. The bear was oddly familiar. That gorgeous fur. Those golden eyes. It was the one that had stalked me when I'd been hiding in the rocky outcropping.

"You were there," I said. "The day with Tomas."

Another nod.

"Were you trying to protect me?" I'd been so scared.

Nod.

I eased forward, hardly able to believe what I was doing. "Can I touch you?"'

He lowered his head to the ground again and made a chuffing sound.

"I'll take that as a yes." I crossed to where he lay and knelt beside him. His nose nudged my hand and I stroked the top of his head, my heart in my throat. He must be able to hear my pulse going crazy, but he seemed to be doing as much as he could to set me at ease.

"Your whole family can do this?" I asked.

He lifted his head again.

"Wow." I shook my head. "I can't believe it."

I was actually sitting beside a bear. Petting him. And I honestly thought he was Everett?

Well, what else was I supposed to think?

"So..." I wondered whether I should keep talking. What was the protocol when the man you were developing feelings for turned into a large, furry predator? "Holy shit." My heart clanked wildly. "I didn't imagine it when I thought Tomas had grown fangs, did I?"

Everett grumbled and moved his head from side to side.

"He's a bear too?"

Everett shuffled away and then seemed to shrink and change form right in front of my eyes until he was kneeling a few feet away from me, completely naked. "He's a wolf."

"A w-wolf?" I balked. "So, it's not just bears out there? People can turn into werewolves too?"

He winced. "We prefer the term 'shifter.' As in, bear shifters and wolf shifters. For pretty much any animal out there, there will be someone who can shift into it, although predator species tend to be more common." He shifted uncomfortably. "In the dark ages, some of our ancestors hunted the smaller, weaker species to extinction, or near extinction."

"Like... like..." My mind filled with horrific images. "Did they eat them?"

"Some clans did. Most didn't, but if they wanted to be the dominant shifter group in an area, they'd take out the others, and it's easier to eliminate weaker species than larger ones."

I could barely process his words. It sounded like some kind of warped history lesson. "Does anyone else in Grizzly Ridge do what you guys do?"

"Almost everyone." He made the statement so factually I wondered why I was surprised. Perhaps I should have guessed that the whole community was in on this. "Most are bear shifters, but we also have a few mountain lions, bobcats, and other species. There haven't been any wolves in the area until lately though."

My gaze wandered over his torso of its own volition. Despite my shock, I could hardly take my eyes off him. He had those broad shoulders, that hairy chest, and the gorgeous cock I wanted to taste again. "Aren't you cold?"

He shrugged. "Shifters run hot, but if it makes you more comfortable, I'll put my clothes on."

"Yes, please," I squeaked. "I can't focus when you're..." I waved a hand at his glorious nakedness, "like that."

His expression turned smug. "Oh, really?"

"As if you don't know how hot you are."

He grinned, and genuine pleasure lit his face. "Always nice to hear it."

I cleared my throat. "Tell me more about the wolves."

"Right." He stood and pulled his clothes on. I watched wistfully as his body disappeared beneath jeans and a hoodie. "A rogue pack has been causing trouble in a neighboring town. We believe Tomas belongs to that pack, but according to their Alpha—their leader—he hasn't been seen recently. Whether that's true, we don't know, but it's possible he's still in Grizzly Ridge. I've caught his scent a couple of times."

"His scent?" I asked, bewildered.

He offered me a hand to pull me to my feet. I took it, noting once again how his hand dwarfed mine. Now, perhaps, I understood his size a bit more. He wasn't just a big guy. He was a literal bear.

"Yeah, bear shifters have an enhanced sense of smell. Once we've smelled someone once, we can identify them again based on their scent."

"So... do I have a scent?"

Heat flared in his eyes, and he leaned close, his nostrils flaring. "You smell absolutely delicious. Like sweet cherries on a spring day."

My dick plumped, and I shivered. How did he make that sound so sensual? "Is that why Tomas tried to bite me? Did he want to eat me?"

He flinched back, his face twisted with horror. "Gods, no."

He hesitated, as if debating how much to reveal.

"Please, Ev," I begged. "I need to know everything. I've been so confused and I thought I was losing my mind."

He pressed his lips together and nodded resolutely.

"Okay." He squared his shoulders. "Every shifter has a mate —or mates—who are their perfect match and made for them in every way. When we find our mate, we claim them with a bite. I believe that's what he was trying to do with you."

"Wait. Hold up." That made no sense. "Why would he think I was his mate?"

Everett scowled. "Fuck if I know. We identify our mates by scent. It's possible that he's feral and made a mistake because of that."

"So, he smelled me, and decided I was his mate?" That explained the sniffing at least. "How do you know I'm not?"

I didn't believe I was the perfect match for a crazy wolf, but how could Everett possibly know Tomas was wrong? Considering I didn't have their sense of smell, surely that meant even I couldn't say it definitively.

Everett placed his hands on my shoulders and looked into my eyes. "Because you're *my* mate."

TWENTY-FOUR

EVERETT

My heart was in my throat as I waited to see how Milo would react. He hadn't run away screaming when I'd shifted, which boded well, but he seemed to be in shock. His eyes were slightly glazed and he kept unconsciously shaking his head.

"I can't be," he said eventually.

"I assure you, you are." The fact my teeth kept dropping and my dick kept hardening when he was around would tell me so, even if his scent hadn't.

"But..." He frowned, as though puzzled. "This is like some weird psychedelic dream. Two supernatural men supposedly think I'm their mate? Not possible. I'm invisible. I'm nothing special. No one ever sees me or wants me."

My jaw clenched. "You're beautiful," I growled.

He looked alarmed, and I forced my bear to calm down.

"Milo," I said softly. "You are the most gorgeous, wonderful, gentle man I've ever met. You're a treasure. You're meant for me. My heart knows it, and my bear does too."

His frown softened, and his eyes shone with hope, but

he bit his lip and looked down. I ground my teeth together. I didn't know how to make him believe me.

"Don't you feel it?" I asked urgently. "The connection? I constantly want to be with you. Touch you. Know everything about you. Being apart from you is excruciating. I just want to kiss you, then bury myself in you and make you mine."

He looked up at me, his pupils massive, and I could smell his arousal. My bear roared internally. He wanted me too. There was no denying it.

"That's what it is?" His voice was quiet. "It's strange, but I felt like I could trust you as soon as I met you, and that never happens with me. Something about being near you reassures me, and yes, I feel the attraction too, but I don't understand how I can be your mate." His mouth turned down. "I'm human."

"Are you?" I asked. "Do you know who your parents are?"

"No." He bit his lip. "But I'm not magical."

"Maybe not," I allowed. "But you could have shifter blood. Or maybe you *are* a human. Mates don't have to be the same species. My mate could be a bear shifter, or a human, or a lion shifter, or a warlock."

"Oh, Gods." Milo leaned against me, and I wrapped my arms around him, inhaling his addictive scent. "Warlocks are a thing? Is that like a male witch?"

"They can be either male or female," I told him. "Warlocks are inherently magical, while witches use potions and poultices. They might have a hint of magic, but usually they fall more in the category of being healers."

"You're serious?" He looked up at me fretfully. "You're not putting me on, are you?"

My eyebrows lowered. "No. I wouldn't do that to you. They exist. Shifters, warlocks, witches, vampires—"

"Vampires?" Now he looked like he might be sick. "Are they around here?"

"We don't have a local coven, but there are a couple of lone vampires in the next town over."

I could smell his fear, and I didn't like it.

"They won't hurt you, baby." Not these, anyway. City vampires tended to be less civilized because it was easier for them to take humans or omegas that nobody would miss.

"I can't believe this." He shoved at my chest, and I reluctantly let him go. He paced around the clearing. "I knew something was off about your family, but I had no idea it was something this massive." His eyes were wild. "These... *beings*... like you. They're all over the world?"

I nodded.

"Holy crap."

Yup, he was realizing the magnitude of the secret that had been kept from him.

"How many of you are there?"

I shrugged. "I don't know. Millions."

"Millions," he repeated weakly.

I tried to pull him into an embrace to comfort him, but he resisted so I let him go. I would never do anything against his will.

"I need to think," he said. "This sounds so crazy." He glanced at me. "I mean, I believe you, because obviously you got furry. But I can't take it all in."

I braced myself. This felt like a rejection. Everything inside me hurt, but it was his right to reject me, and if he did, I'd honor that. But then his expression softened and he took my hand. I held my body still as he raised my hand to his lips and kissed the back of it. I ached to take him in my arms, but he clearly didn't want that.

"It's a lot," he explained. "I need time to understand what it means."

A little of the fear seeped away. He wasn't rejecting me. At least not outright.

"Okay. I respect that. How about we walk back and I'll answer any questions you have along the way?"

CHAPTER
TWENTY-FIVE

MILO

I was on a one-way voyage to crazy town. There was no other explanation for the fact I honestly believed that Everett—and apparently his whole family—could turn into a bear at will, and that I was somehow destined to be his perfect match. His *mate*.

It was insane... wasn't it? Then why did I crave everything he'd said about being mated? Having one person who was made for me and who loved me more than anything sounded like a dream I'd never dared to have. But I'd learned that if things sounded too good to be true, they usually were.

As we started walking, I wondered what to ask Everett first. I had so many questions, and I knew that the more the truth sank in, the more I'd have.

"So, do shifters mate instead of getting married?" I asked.

Everett turned toward me. I felt his big frame move, and I longed to press myself against his side or to let him hold me in his arms again, but this world I'd stumbled into wasn't something I could pretend didn't exist just by wrapping him around me as a shield.

"Yes." His voice was gruff. "Although some shifters get married so that their relationship is legitimate in the eyes of the human government."

My eyes widened. "What do you mean 'the human government'? Is there a shifter government too?"

"Not exactly." The back of his hand brushed mine. "We have a council where a member of each species is put forward as a representative to vote on important matters and participate in political discussions."

"Huh." Somehow my first thought had been that this new world was dangerous and chaotic, but it would seem I'd had that wrong.

"Anyway," Everett continued. "Back to the mating versus marriage discussion. The connections are different in that once a couple is mated, a bond is formed between them forever. The bond can weaken, but it's never gone."

I frowned. That sounded intense. "What type of bond?"

"It allows mates to sense each other's emotions, and sometimes experience them. Very rarely, mates are able to communicate telepathically. Usually during times of high stress."

"Wow." My mind immediately flashed to some of the couples I'd lived with, and I couldn't help thinking how much shorter their marriages might have been if they'd known what the other was thinking. "So, there's no equivalent of divorce."

Everett hesitated. After a pause, he said, "Not without invoking dark magic."

I shook my head instinctively. Dark magic? If he'd talked to me like this when I'd first turned up in town, I'd have run screaming for the nearest cab back to the city—even if I'd had to travel half the way on foot. But after seeing him morph from human to bear and back again, I was inclined to take him at his word.

I bit my lip, knowing he wouldn't like my next question, but it had to be asked. After all, Tomas hadn't cared about my opinion and in some societies, omegas were considered possessions. There was no reason to think the same wasn't true in his world.

"Do both partners have a say in the mating?"

He stopped abruptly and a growl tore through him. When I spun to face him, hurt was etched in every line of his face. I reached for him, but he stepped away and my hand fell to my side.

"You can choose not to mate with me," he rasped. "I would never, ever force you. But if you reject me, then I'll never mate. You're the only one for me."

My heart gave an extra thump. I stared at him, hardly able to believe my ears. "So... what? You'd just be alone forever?"

His eyes were sad. "Another shifter in my place might choose a partner in their mate's stead, but it wouldn't be the same. And for me after having met you, there's no going back."

My stomach squeezed at the pain in his expression. I hated that I'd put it there. I hadn't meant to hurt him, but I needed to understand.

"If you get to know me better, you'll see how perfect we are for each other." His tone was low but pleading. "I would do anything for you. I swear it."

How was I supposed to resist that?

I went to him and cupped his bearded face between my hands. "I'm sorry. I didn't mean to upset you."

I kissed him. For a moment, he stood stiff with shock, but then every muscle in his body seemed to bunch at once and he grabbed me, pivoted, and pressed me against a tree.

He held me in place with his hand at the back of my neck and deepened the kiss, his tongue tangling with mine. He ate at me, ravenous, and I tried to climb his body and wrap my arms around his lean hips.

He pulled back, and his eyes were gold. I realized now that I hadn't been imagining things all those times when I thought something was off about his eyes. It was his bear peeking through at me. His lips parted and sharp teeth showed between them. He panted, and after a moment, his eyes changed back and the teeth withdrew.

"You're beautiful," I whispered. Perhaps I should be scared by the beast within him, but it didn't feel dangerous to me. In fact, I got the impression he and his bear would tear anyone to shreds if they dared touch me. To someone raised in a nuclear family, that might be a red flag, but to me and my needy heart, it was everything.

His expression softened. "Yeah?"

"Mm-hmm." I pressed a soft kiss against his lips, drawing away before he could pounce again. I placed my hands over his chest and gazed up at him. "Does it hurt? Mating, I mean."

Everett considered the question. "From what I understand, it's a bit like sex. There's a temporary discomfort but then the bond forms and pleasure takes over."

His mouth curved up and his expression became one of longing. He wanted that. With me. But it was a massive commitment, and the whole mate thing was new to me. I couldn't just let him do it because I didn't want him to be unhappy. We would literally be bound together for life, and I hardly knew him. He was sexy and protective, and I was drawn to him like no one else, but he was still, in essence, a stranger.

"It sounds nice," I admitted. "But I'm not ready for that yet. I need time."

Everett held me close, cupping my head against his chest. I buried my face in his shirt and breathed him in.

"I can give you time. And don't worry about Tomas. The wolf isn't getting his hands on you."

I shivered. I believed him, but at the end of the day, Tomas wasn't human. I was being hunted by someone who had the ability to turn into a giant wolf, and that was terrifying.

TWENTY-SIX

EVERETT

After our outing into the woods, I returned Milo to my parents' place. We found Momma and Dad at the breakfast nook in the kitchen. The remains of their breakfast had already been tidied away, and Dad was flicking through paperwork of some form while Momma decorated gingerbread men—presumably for the children's home.

"Good morning," I called as we entered. Milo stuck close to my side. His discovery seemed to have made him less certain of his welcome.

"It's so good to see you," Momma said, standing to give Milo a hug. He accepted the gesture but didn't seem to enjoy it the way I'd noticed he usually did. "How are you today?"

He stared at her as if he didn't understand the question, but then seemed to come back to himself. "Oh, I'm fine."

"Are you sure?" Her forehead furrowed with concern. "You must have gotten quite a scare yesterday. No one would blame you if you felt off today."

"Erm, um." He looked at me for help, and I could hear

the pounding of his heart. I wished my revelation hadn't changed anything between us, but it seemed to, even if it was only temporary. Some of his original wariness had reared its head.

I sighed. "He got another scare this morning." I met Momma's eyes and then Dad's. "I told him. And showed him."

"Ah." She didn't sound surprised, which meant she'd either suspected I would or Dad had let her know my intentions. "Well, I'm glad we can be completely honest with you now."

Milo gave a faltering smile. "Me too."

To my surprise, Dad patted the stool beside him, indicating for Milo to take it, and said, "We're sorry for any confusion you've felt over the past few days. It's not something we can tell just anyone."

"Of course not," Milo said faintly as he sat on the stool. "It's good to know I haven't gone crazy. I kinda wondered for a while."

"You're not crazy," I assured him, upset that he'd doubted himself. "You're smart and perceptive. Other humans have stayed for longer without noticing anything out of the ordinary." I walked up behind him and pressed myself to his back. To my delight, he relaxed against me, soft and pliant. My chest puffed out. I was honored he would show me that trust. It was unexpected.

Milo cleared his throat. "So, you're shifters."

"That's right." Dad watched him closely, as if looking for a hint he might be about to announce our existence to the world.

"And most of the town are shifters, or shifter-adjacent?"

I chuckled at his choice of words, but he wasn't wrong. "Yes."

He glanced at the gingerbread men that Momma was decorating. "What about the kids from the home?"

"Also shifters," Momma said gently. "Would you like to know what type?"

Milo chewed on his lip, clearly thinking it over.

I massaged his shoulders. "You can say no," I murmured. "We don't want to overload you with information too fast."

"No." He raised his chin. "I'd like to know, please, Melinda."

Momma smiled. "Wonderful. Little Lacey and her brother are squirrels. Sam is a fox. The other girls are all bears."

Milo shook his head, looking dazed. "Now there's something I never expected to hear."

My parents exchanged a worried look. They were concerned he was overwhelmed and would out us all, but I knew they didn't need to be. My Milo was stronger than that.

"Why don't I take Milo for a walk around town?" I suggested. "I can show him everything properly and answer any of his questions."

Milo stiffened. He tilted his head back to look up at me. "Is it safe?"

I mentally cursed at myself. I should have realized he'd be more afraid of the wolf now that he knew what he was. I opened my mouth to reply, but Dad beat me to it.

"Everett is one of our best fighters," he said. "You'll be safe with him."

Milo's face scrunched and he pushed me away, then spun to face me properly. "What do you mean, one of the best fighters?"

The question may have been in response to my father, but I knew it was directed at me.

"We may be a peaceful clan, but we still need people to keep order and who can protect us if needed," I explained. "I'm one of the clan's enforcers, which means I've been trained to fight in both my human and bear forms."

Not that the bear required much training. It operated more on instinct.

His lower lip wobbled. "But... but I don't want you to get hurt because of me."

My bear bristled at the idea that our mate believed another shifter might be able to overpower us.

Calm down, I told him. *He hasn't seen you in action.*

The human side of me was flattered that Milo wanted me to be safe, even if I agreed with my bear that it was unnecessary.

"You have absolutely nothing to worry about," I said. "Nothing will happen to me or you."

"You can't promise that," he whispered.

He was right, but I wished he wasn't.

"Trust me."

"Okay." When he stood and put his hand in mine, I felt like a king.

TWENTY-SEVEN

MILO

I had a vague sense of deja vu as Everett and I walked into the township of Grizzly Ridge. Just yesterday, I'd made this same journey with his brother, and it had ended poorly. But Everett told me we were safe for now, and I believed him. Whether or not I was fully on board with the mate thing, he was, and I knew he'd never do anything to endanger me. Unfortunately, that didn't stop me from worrying about what would happen if he was called on to fight to protect me, as his dad had insinuated. Everett was a good man. Caring and kind. I didn't want him to get hurt because of me.

"Are they bears?" I asked, gesturing at a nearby family to distract myself. There was an alpha and an omega in their thirties with a little girl swinging between them.

"They are," he said. "That's the Trevors family."

I glanced at a pair of teenage boys. "What about them?"

He nodded. "Also bears. Most of the people who live here are, although we have a few exceptions."

I frowned, thinking of the children from the group home. Squirrels, bears, and foxes. Crazy. Although come to think of it, Sam did resemble a fox with their clever, narrow face, and Lacey had been peppy and fun.

"What about George?" I asked. "The man who manages the group home."

Everett smiled. "Now he's something else entirely."

"What?" I demanded. "Warlock? Witch? Vampire?"

He chuckled. "No. Human."

"Oh." Why did I find that disappointing?

We continued a circuit through the township, and Everett pointed out things he thought might be of interest. When he'd apparently reached the end of the guided tour, he led me back to the cafe on the main street. It was a charming little place. Warm inside, with a red-and-white checkered pattern on one wall and the day's menu written on a chalkboard.

"What would you like?" Everett asked as we joined the line.

I started to scan the options, but stopped when I realized I'd garnered the attention of the alpha in front of us. He leered at me with a level of interest that made me squirm.

"Who's the pretty omega?" he asked Everett. "Aren't you going to introduce us?"

I flattened myself against Everett's side. I didn't think the alpha was dangerous, but I didn't like the way he looked at me like I was a snack. What was it with the men around here? In the city I couldn't find an alpha who'd look at me twice, and here I was getting more attention than I wanted.

Everett growled. Not just a mild grumble, but a throaty warning that must have originated from the creature who lived within him.

The alpha backed off, his hands raised. "Whoa. Sorry, man. I didn't realize he was yours."

I noticed him glance down at my neck and I self-consciously tugged at my collar. Was he checking for a mating bite? Was that something shifters did to ascertain whether an omega was single, like looking for wedding rings on humans? I chanced a look at Everett and found him watching me with soft eyes.

"Sorry about that," he said. "He won't bother you again."

My eyes widened. He thought that was the most note-worthy part of what had happened. "What was with the growl?"

To my surprise, his cheeks colored. "My bear is territorial when it comes to you. It sees another alpha expressing interest as a challenge."

My heart did an uncomfortable flip and my stomach fluttered. "Nobody has ever been possessive of me before."

He slanted me a look. "You don't mind?"

"I don't." In fact, I was amazed at how much I didn't mind. I loved the idea that he was willing to make a scene over me, even if I didn't want it to actually happen. "You talk about your bear as if he's separate from you. Aren't you the same being?"

The line moved forward and Everett shifted with it as he looked down at me thoughtfully.

"The bear is part of me, and human Everett is part of me," he said after a moment. "It's as if we're two sides of the same coin. We share a spirit, but we're not one. Some-times we disagree. It's like having a particularly feral and loud voice in the back of my mind, and sometimes, he takes over. In those instances, I'm still me, but everything is sharper. My instincts are more primal. Human logic makes less sense."

"Intriguing." I mulled it over while the lady at the counter took our orders, then Everett escorted us to a small table in the corner. "I can't imagine what that must be like."

Everett took my hand. He seemed to do it automatically, and the action warmed my heart. "You'll find out if we mate."

My stomach tingled. "What do you mean?"

He tore a piece off his pastry and chewed it. "You remember how I said that mates can sense each other's emotions? That goes for both me and my bear. If we mate, you'll be able to sense and communicate with both parts of me."

"That sounds nice." I'd never been close to someone before. I'd never even had a best friend, let alone a boyfriend. I couldn't fathom how being that deeply connected to someone would feel. To have that tangible proof you belonged with them. I yearned for it. I was beginning to think that whatever Everett was, and however intimidating the prospect of mating might be, perhaps it was the answer to everything I'd ever wanted.

TWENTY-EIGHT

EVERETT

At dusk, the clan gathered in our meeting place on the edge of the woods behind the Alpha's house. Dad sat at a chair atop the deck while the rest of the clan, excluding Zander, his Beta, assembled on the lawn. Some were in their human forms, but others had shifted— perhaps to ward off the cold. Milo hovered at my side, his delicious scent soured by a tinge of fear.

I wished he wasn't afraid of us, but I understood it. He'd only learned about us this morning and now we were all around him. He had a right to be wary—especially since some clan members might not approve of one of the Alpha's sons mating with a human. As with any community, there were bigots. Some shifters believed our kind should only mate with shifters, or with our own particular species of shifter. I thought it was bullshit. If the Gods hadn't wanted me to have a human mate, the fates wouldn't have bestowed one on me.

"Attention," Dad called, his booming Alpha voice in full force. "I've called you here because there's a threat we need everyone to be aware of."

Whispers broke out, and a few clan members looked scared while others puffed their chests as if to show that they were ready to defend our home.

"A rogue wolf pack has been living in the area for a couple of months, and yesterday, they tried to abduct someone from within Grizzly Ridge territory," he continued.

I heard gasps and cursing.

Dad waved a hand toward Milo. "This is Milo Silva. He was walking home from the bakery when an omega asked for his assistance with a van. When Milo approached, an alpha attacked him."

More gasps. My hands tightened into fists and my bear seethed. Milo leaned against my side. I exhaled gently and forced myself not to shift and let my bear wreak havoc on the rogue wolf pack like he wanted to.

"When questioned, we discovered that the omega had been taken from his hometown against his will and was being used by the pack as a laborer."

I quietly hoped that was all he'd been used for. Rogue alphas could be violent and some believed they had an inherent right to any omega they wanted.

"The alpha hasn't said anything useful. He's been transferred to the state holding facility where he'll face a charge of assault and attempted kidnapping." Dad growled in a way that made me think he wished we could have dealt with the wolf the old-fashioned way. "In the meantime, I want you all to be on the lookout for wolves in the area."

A hand went up. I squinted to see who it was and groaned.

"Yes, John?" Dad's mouth turned down at the corners.

"I heard that the wolf was only trying to collect his mate," John called. He was an overweight guy in his forties who made up part of the older faction and believed that omegas were possessions rather than people.

"You heard incorrectly." Dad's expression didn't waver.

"How do we know?" John persisted. "The omega could be lying."

A sea of faces turned toward Milo. I sensed him trying to hide behind me and I clutched his hand, squeezing it gently to show my support.

I cleared my throat. "For one thing, Milo doesn't have a mating bite, and for another, he's my fated mate."

A murmur rose from the group. I heard a couple of muttered comments about how inappropriate it was for the Alpha's son to be with a human, but thankfully they were quiet enough that I doubted Milo noticed. John stared at me in horror. I narrowed my eyes and stared right back. If he wanted to make a scene, he'd have to think about it really damn carefully because I would defend my mate. Milo had been rejected enough. He didn't need bigots like John adding to the ranks of those who made him feel like he didn't matter.

Dad called the clan to order. "Are there any other questions?" Nobody raised their hand. "Good." His expression was dangerous. "Then let's close the meeting and run together."

TWENTY-NINE

MILO

Even if I couldn't hear what they were saying, it was clear that not everyone here approved of me. A couple of people, including the one who'd suggested I might be a liar, looked at me with outright hostility. I tried to focus on the others, some of whom were smiling, but my tendency toward caution outweighed my desire to avoid unpleasantness. I kept an eye on the hostile ones in case I needed to run for my life. If they came after me in their other forms, there wouldn't be anything I could do to defend myself.

"It's okay," Everett said, pinning me to his side. "I've got you. You're safe here. Remember, they're still cognizant after they've shifted."

I blinked, taking a moment to realize that he was talking about the fact that the clan members who hadn't already shifted into their animal form were now stripping off their clothes. Somehow I'd tuned it out, but now that he'd drawn my attention, I couldn't ignore the nudity. My cheeks heated and I dropped my head to look at the ground.

"Is this normal?" I asked. "You all just get naked with each other?"

I felt him shrug. "Nudity isn't a big deal for us. Unless we want to spend a fortune in clothes, we have to strip every time we shift, so we're used to it."

I glanced up at him, imagining the others around us seeing his broad, hairy chest and thick cock. I frowned. "I'd rather keep your body to myself."

At least there was no reason for me to get naked too. Even the other omegas seemed bigger and stronger than me. I couldn't imagine I'd measure up. I squirmed in discomfort, wondering how many of the local shifters Everett might have hooked up with in the past. I couldn't help but feel like he must wish I were more like them, no matter what he said to the contrary. It would be difficult for him to have a scrawny human mate.

"Hey." Everett pressed my head to his chest, encouraging me to lean against him. "What's wrong?"

"Nothing," I mumbled. "Just being an insecure mess, like usual."

"You've got nothing to be insecure about." He put a finger beneath my chin and tipped my head up. His eyes were on mine, tender and dark. They flashed gold. "You are the most beautiful man I've ever known, inside and out." He pressed a gentle kiss to my lips. "No matter how many people see me naked, I'll only want you."

I felt warm and gooey inside. For the first time, I believed him all the way to my core. He cared about me not just as his fated mate, but because he liked me as a person. For some reason, that distinction felt important.

I snuggled closer, burrowing into his arms, but then jerked in surprise as something snuffled from a few feet away. I spun around and my eyes widened at the sight of a large bear waiting for us to finish canoodling.

"Danny," Everett said.

I studied the bear closely. I had to admit, I could see no trace of Everett's brother, but the bear's eyes were gentle as he moved toward me slowly. When he drew near enough to touch, he nuzzled my abdomen. Tentatively, I stroked him. He backed away and bared his teeth in a frightening smile, then turned and lumbered away to join the others. Seeing him beside some of the alpha bears, I realized he wasn't actually that big. Closer in stature to a normal grizzly, while some of the others were much larger.

"Are you going to join them?" I asked Everett.

"No." He kissed the top of my head. "I'm staying with you until we know you're safe."

I grimaced, hating that he had to give something up because of me. If we stayed together, would he become less connected with his family because of how I held him back? I felt sick at the thought.

"I don't mind if you go. I'm sure I'll be safe here." With so many shifters around, surely no one would be able to sneak up undetected.

"Milo, I'm not going." He ruffled my hair. "I'd rather hold you anyway."

I hesitated, still feeling guilty about the situation. But there was at least one thing I could offer him that might make up for it in part. "Can I spend time with your bear again?"

He looked pleased. "I'd love that."

When he started stripping off, I positioned myself between him and everyone else. Yes, they'd no doubt seen him in all his glory a dozen times before, but he was mine now. Or he would be if I decided to go ahead with this mating thing.

Everett put some space between us and I watched, completely in awe, as he sprouted fur and grew into a hulking form. The bear dropped his front paws to the ground and cocked his head inquisitively. I approached him with a hand out, and he nudged it with his nose.

Another alpha in human form approached, and Everett growled.

"Hi." The man smiled at me but kept a respectful distance, giving Everett a side-eye. "I'm Yuri. I work with Ev. I'd like to welcome you to the clan. Everett has been ready for his mate for a while, and I'm happy he's found you."

Everett huffed and bumped Yuri's leg. Yuri raised an eyebrow but didn't touch him.

"Thank you." I smiled back. It was nice to know at least some clan members didn't resent my presence. "It's nice to meet you."

He waved toward a slim man with shiny black hair that I only now noticed was hovering a few yards behind him. "This is my mate, Li. He's not a shifter."

"He's human?" I asked.

"No." Li himself spoke as he came forward, keeping a wary eye on Everett. "I'm a witch, although my gift is limited to healing poultices and the occasional energy transfer."

"You're still more interesting than me," I pointed out. "I'm as human as they get." Once again, I wondered whether that would bother Everett.

Li smiled crookedly. "I definitely wouldn't consider you to be boring, Milo. If this wolf shifter has fixated on you, there must be something to it."

I shrugged, feeling like a fraud because there really wasn't.

"We're going to join the run now," Yuri said. "We look forward to seeing more of you though."

"Thank you. Have fun."

I watched them leave, but turned away as they started removing clothes. Everett lay down and made a motion with his arm that I didn't understand. He repeated it. Perhaps he was asking me to join him. I went to him and sat on the edge of the deck. He wrapped himself around me like a big, furry comforter. I rested my head on him and listened to the sound of his breath as the grunts faded away. It was lovely to exist with him like this, beneath a night blanketed with stars and the solid strength of his body surrounding me.

We stayed that way until the clan members began to return. Everett shifted and dressed.

"Would you like to stay at my place tonight?" he asked, looking unusually vulnerable.

I kissed his chest. "Yes, I want to be with you."

THIRTY

EVERETT

My hard, throbbing cock nestled between the plump cheeks of Milo's ass. I gritted my teeth and fought the urge to bury myself inside him. He was asleep. He didn't know how badly I wanted him each time he murmured and wriggled his peachy ass against my hard-on. The faint scent of slick made it harder to resist. Even if he wasn't conscious of it, his body was getting ready for me. He wriggled again, and I growled under my breath.

Claim.

My bear didn't understand the delay.

Claim. Mate. Ours.

He was frustrated, and he wasn't the only one. I needed to get out of here before I lost control and did something I couldn't take back. I tried to disentangle myself from Milo, but he clung to me. I uncurled his fingers from my arm and eased away. I'd nearly made it to the edge of the bed when Milo's eyes fluttered open.

"You're leaving?" He sounded hurt.

My bear was simmering beneath the surface, mad at me

for upsetting our mate, and still confused as to why I hadn't given him a mating bite.

"I need a minute to get myself under control." My voice was a rumble. "My bear is too close. I need to put some distance between us so I can calm down."

To my utter shock, Milo pouted. "But I don't want you to get yourself under control."

He threw a leg across my waist and straddled me. His hands came to my chest. Groaning, I collapsed back against the mattress.

"Fuck."

Sweet Milo was straddling my hard cock. He seemed to realize it at the same time I did. His eyes widened and he shifted his hips experimentally.

"Oh," he said breathlessly.

"Yeah, 'oh,'" I ground out. "Unless you want to test me, you need to move."

He caught his lip between his teeth, and his pupils dilated. "What if I want to test you?"

I closed my eyes. What had I done to deserve this torture? "Then you'd better be prepared for the consequences."

He rolled his hips, grinding against me. The scent of his slick thickened in the air.

"I want them." He moved sinuously against me. "I've never felt like this, Ev. I've never wanted anyone so badly. You're all I can think of."

I opened my eyes, my chest puffing with pride. Milo was still moving above me, his cheeks flushed a delicious shade of pink, his eyes dark with desire. "I'm not mating you." I wouldn't allow him to make an irreversible decision when he was worked up like this. "But I'll take the edge off. Do you trust me, baby?"

He smiled more openly than I'd ever seen him smile

before. My heart expanded and filled with emotion. "More than anyone."

"Let me take care of you." I lifted him off me, ignoring his protest, and stripped off my underwear, which was beginning to constrict my dick too much. Milo sighed happily and reached for it but I tutted. "No touching. We're focusing on you."

I wrapped one hand around his pretty cock and stroked the length of it. He whimpered and thrust into my grip, precum easing the way.

"Have you ever had anything in your ass before?" I asked him. "Have you used toys or fingered yourself?"

His flush deepened. "No."

He looked shy, and I didn't want him in any doubt about how much I valued all the firsts he was giving me.

"Then my finger is going to be the first inside your tight hole. Would you like that, baby?"

"Yes," he whispered. "Please, Ev. I'm so turned on."

"I know. I've got you." I released his cock and claimed his mouth instead, tasting him, relaxing him. While he was distracted, I slipped my hand underneath him and brushed a finger over his hole. It was already soft, slick, and slightly open. I petted the rim and, when the remaining tension eased from his muscles, I pushed past the outer muscles and into his scalding heat. I paused, giving him a moment to adjust. "Okay?"

His eyes met mine, glazed and unfocused. "More."

I kissed his hip. "We'll go slow. If you don't like anything, tell me to stop."

He started to roll his eyes but I crooked my finger and brushed his prostate. He gasped and stared at me, wide-eyed. I rubbed the spot again and his head fell back. He groaned, and his dick pulsed.

I grinned. "Ah, you like that, don't you, baby?"

"P-Please." He moved restlessly, trying to fuck himself on my finger.

I shifted until I was at eye-level with his pretty cock and took it down my throat. His salty taste filled my mouth and his hips jerked instinctively. I sucked and licked, never stopping the slow back-and-forth of my finger over his gland. He swore and writhed and panted. His dick was throbbing steel, and I could tell he was close to the edge. I pulled off him and started pumping him with my other hand.

"Come," I ordered. "I want to see you lose it, omega. Tell me I'm the only one who'll ever see you come."

"Only you, alpha," he groaned. "My alpha."

Fuck, yeah. I liked being his.

I suckled on the juicy head of his cock. He wailed and bucked, helpless noises spilling from his lips as he came in my mouth. I swallowed and eased my finger from him, then shuffled up the bed and clasped him to me.

"Kiss?" he asked.

I smiled fondly. I had a feeling my omega would be filthy in bed once he gained more confidence. I kissed him, sharing his taste, but drew back as my fangs started to descend. He whined in protest.

"Easy, baby," I soothed. "My bear wants to bite you."

"Yeah?" Something unfamiliar sparkled in his eyes. "Well, I want to make you come."

"Milo..." I feared if he came near my erection, I'd bite him and to hell with the consequences.

"I need to," he insisted, his pale blue eyes determined. "You keep making me come and I want to do the same for you."

"We're not keeping score," I told him.

"I know." He licked his lower lip. "But I want to drive you crazy, the same way you do to me. I want to feel you let go."

I studied his beloved face. I wanted to give him what he asked for, but there were risks. "If I lose control, I can't promise I won't bite you."

His smile lit me up inside. "I trust you."

Ah, fuck. I was a goner.

"Okay, then, baby." I lay back and spread my arms. "I'm all yours."

He scanned my body with a hunger that made me feel like I was an all-you-can-eat buffet. His gaze locked on my cock, and for a moment, I thought he was going to blow me again. But then he knelt over me, reached behind himself, and I heard the obscene sound of his fingers in his own slick.

My breathing grew heavy. "Baby, what are you doing?"

"Playing." His smile was heartbreakingly beautiful. "You don't mind, do you?"

Mind? I bit my lower lip. This man was going to be the death of me.

"Whatever you want."

I wasn't expecting him to straddle me again, but when he did, he positioned himself so my aching cock was sandwiched between his cheeks as it had been while we slept. He rested his hands on my chest and began to ride me, rubbing his crease along the length of my dick. He must have spread his slick because he glided easily from root to tip, and delight gleamed in his pale eyes.

"Do you like that?" he asked.

"It's perfect, baby." I grabbed his hips, unable to help myself, and guided his movements, using him to work myself. He didn't seem to mind the manhandling. In fact, based on the way his cock plumped slightly, he liked it.

"I want to make you come so hard you never think of another man again." His words were breathy and the possessive note sent sparks flying down my spine.

"I won't," I vowed. "You don't have to do anything to prove yourself."

His hips moved faster and he threw his head back, his cock nearly hard again as it slapped against his abdomen.

"Oh, fuck." My gaze locked on the creamy, unmarred skin of his shoulder. My teeth sharpened and grew.

When Milo cried out, another spurt of come shot from his dick and splattered across my stomach and his lean torso. I stared at his face, afraid to miss a second of him taking his bliss. His mouth opened wide and his pupils bled into his blue irises. The visual was overwhelming, especially when the sharp tang of his seed was all I could smell.

"I'm gonna come," I warned.

"Give it to me," he demanded.

Bossy little thing. I loved it.

I thrust against him once more, then shuddered as my load spilled into his crease. He kept riding me until the last of my shivers had passed. He flopped onto my chest, come gluing us together, but I didn't make any effort to move him. I wanted all the cuddles he had to give.

Bite.

Not yet, I told my bear. But soon.

THIRTY-ONE

MILO

After starting the day with orgasms, Everett and I joined his family for breakfast at his parents' house. I didn't miss the sidelong glances, and I wondered whether they'd guessed what Everett and I had been up to. My cheeks flamed at the thought, but I was also secretly proud. I wanted people to know Everett was with me. I wanted to be seen with him and to have everyone know he was off the market. Mine.

I'd never been jealous or possessive before, but I'd been quietly disappointed earlier when I'd had to wash his come off before we left his place. I would have loved to rub it into my skin and carry his scent with me all day. Filthy, perhaps, but I was discovering I contained multitudes.

I scooped a spoonful of mixture out of the food processor and rolled it between my palms. Now that breakfast was over, Melinda and I were making food for the children's home. She was baking a fruit crumble while I prepared what she called bliss balls. The balls were a combination of ground nuts and dried fruit, with a bit of honey for sweetness. My hands were coated in gunk but I was smiling while Melinda sang along to a song on the radio.

I felt like I was doing something useful for once. I'd never realized how much happier I was when I believed I might be making a positive difference, even in a small way. I didn't have that in the city. My job was important, but at the end of the day, it was just moving money around to make rich people richer. That couldn't possibly compare to making food for children who didn't have anyone else to feed or love them.

Everett stood beside me, grumbling as he rolled balls. He'd cracked a few jokes about nuts and balls at the beginning, but now he'd fallen into a contemplative silence. I was curious what he was thinking about, but I wouldn't ask in front of Melinda.

When he'd announced he was staying home to keep an eye on me, I'd half-heartedly protested, but honestly, I was grateful for his presence. Having his solid body next to mine made me feel safe in a way I wouldn't have if it were just Melinda and me. I knew Everett would protect me. I'd seen him do it. And no matter how much I might pretend to be strong, I was scared. I was just a human, and an omega at that. Tomas was an alpha wolf shifter, who apparently had help from some kind of rogue pack—I didn't really know what that meant, except that Tomas wasn't the only one who might be out to get me. Having Everett around soothed my anxiety.

I grabbed the last of the mixture out of the food processor and pressed it into a ball. "That's all of them."

"Great timing," Melinda said. "The crumble is ready to go too."

Everett sighed. "Are you sure the kids really need it? You know I love a good crumble."

"Yes, Ev," she said sternly. "But I know you're a devil

when it comes to crumble, so there's a second one in the warmer for tonight."

Everett kissed her cheek. "Best Momma ever."

Melinda waved him off, but I could tell the comment pleased her. To me, she really did seem like the best mom ever. Warm, caring, and an excellent cook. I was jealous she wasn't mine.

We made our way to the group home and this time, it was George who opened the door. He smiled in greeting, and I couldn't help but have a whole new level of respect for him. I had no idea how one small human could possibly wrangle a group of supernatural children. He must be like Mary Poppins. I'd once watched that film at a foster home and dreamed of a Mary Poppins rescuing me.

"Hello, Melinda," George said. "Milo, it's good to see you again, and Everett, what a surprise."

Everett grunted. "I visit sometimes."

"So you do," George said agreeably. "I hear you're in on the town's secret now, Milo. The children will be so pleased they can show you their counterparts."

"I look forward to seeing them." For once, the thought of seeing shifters in their other form didn't make me nervous. The children would be smaller and cuter. I could work with that.

George stepped back so we could enter but gestured for us to wait. "Sam."

I glanced down and noticed a small, wiry fox at his feet. I knelt and held out a hand to Sam. Everett had told me it was all right to do this, but that I should never pet a shifter without their permission. Sam crept forward and sniffed my hand, then put their paws on my knees and gazed up at my face.

"Hi there," I said. "You're magnificent."

Sam preened. They darted a look over their shoulder

and slunk away as a pair of fluffy squirrels raced down the hall toward us. I laughed with delight and held out a hand the same way I had with Sam. The smaller squirrel ran up my arm and perched on my shoulder. Grinning, I met Everett's eyes. They were soft and full of affection.

"Do you want to get down again?" I asked the squirrel, but they shook their head.

"That one is Lacey," Melinda said. "Abel is more shy."

I smiled at the other squirrel and my stomach buzzed with happiness. Adults were overwhelming, but I could manage kids. "Come on, Lacey. We've got a delicious lunch for you."

She chattered with excitement.

"I think you've got a new fan," Everett murmured.

My heart swelled. "I'd like that."

WE LEFT the children's home, waving goodbye to Lacey and Abel while Sam watched from a bedroom window. Everett wrapped his arm around me and kissed my forehead.

"You're amazing with those kids," he said.

I shrugged. "I grew up around kids. Even in foster homes, it was never just me. Granted, not all of them were nice, but even then I could relate to what they were going through. We were all in a shitty situation and making the best of it the only way we knew how."

Everett stopped walking and drew me into his embrace. I buried my face against his chest and soaked up his strength. Melinda continued on, giving us privacy.

"I'm sorry you had a crappy childhood," he said gruffly. "And that you never had a home, but you have one here. You're wanted and needed. You belong with me."

I blinked rapidly as tears sprang to my eyes. "Shut up," I mutter half-heartedly. "You're going to make me cry."

"It's just the truth, baby." He drew back and peppered my face with kisses. "You're the other half of myself, and even though we haven't known each other long, I'd fall apart without you."

I smiled tentatively. Perhaps some people would see that as a red flag, or a sign they should run screaming, but to me it sounded pretty damn good. Maybe I should be brave and give this mating thing a shot.

THIRTY-TWO

MILO

When we got back to Melinda's place, she told us we might as well make ourselves useful and gave us a shopping list and instructions to go to the store. We walked back to the center of town. The local grocery store was a charming wooden building with big windows that overlooked a sports field. As we entered, I grabbed a basket but Everett laughed and took it off me, returning it to the holder and pulling out a cart instead.

"Trust me, we'll need it," he said.

We passed a couple of people I recognized from last night, including the red-faced John, who was stamped in my mind because of his insulting suggestion that I was lying about being mated. How could I be lying about that when I hadn't even known mating was a thing until now? He didn't smile at me, and I didn't smile at him.

We worked our way through the shop aisle by aisle. When we were done, we lined up at the checkout. I glanced down at the list and realized we'd missed the flour. It had been written closely beneath another item and I hadn't seen it there.

"Hold on," I said to Everett. "I need to get some flour. I'll just be a moment."

I navigated back through the aisles, finding the baking goods easily. I grabbed the flour and turned to go, but a voice made me stop in my tracks. I recognized it instantly as John's.

"It's not right," he said to his companion. "The Alpha's sons should mate with other shifters."

"I can't believe the Alpha is allowing it," his companion said. "Diluting the bloodlines. Next thing you know, he'll be sanctioning vampire-shifter matings."

John made a sound of disgust. "Everyone needs to keep to their own damn kind."

My heart sank. The back of my throat tightened and I somehow managed to walk to the checkout with my head held high, but I felt like crying. Did the rest of the clan feel the same way those men did? I'd sensed some unease at the meeting last night, but I'd got the impression most of the shifters were friendly. Perhaps I'd been wrong, and they all secretly wished I'd go back to where I belonged.

Which was where, exactly? I'd never belonged anywhere in my life.

"Hey, what's wrong?" Everett asked as I approached.

"Nothing." I dropped the flour onto the checkout belt and tried to smile.

"Are you sure?" He clearly didn't believe me, but I wasn't going to admit that his own clan members, or whatever the heck they were called, didn't want me there. If he knew that, he might send me away. After all, these were his people. His community. I was just some guy he'd met a few days ago.

You're his mate, a voice in my mind said. I ignored it.

We didn't talk much on the way home. As we unpacked, I got the feeling Everett wanted to pull me aside and demand to know what had happened, but Danny arrived for lunch before he got the chance.

"I brought sandwiches," Danny said, handing one to me and two to Everett.

"Thanks." His thoughtfulness lifted my spirits a little.

"You're welcome." He glanced from Everett to me and his eyes narrowed. "Is everything okay here?"

"Something is wrong with Milo, but he won't tell me what," Everett groused.

"Ah." Danny sounded as if that explained it all.

"How was the bakery this morning?" I asked, desperate for a distraction.

Danny launched into a story about a particularly difficult customer, and I relaxed. But when Everett excused himself to use the bathroom, Danny cut off speaking midstream.

He leaned closer. "Okay, here's what you need to know about Ev," he said quickly. "He always wants to protect everyone. Recently, I had a boyfriend who... well, he was an abusive asshole. I hid it from Ev and the rest of my family. He only found out when he caught my ex kicking the shit out of me."

My heart ached and I stared at him in shock. "Gods, I'm so sorry. Why are you telling me this?"

It was difficult to imagine Danny as a victim. He seemed so confident and comfortable with himself. And really, it was none of my business. I didn't understand his urgency to share it with me.

"Because not knowing what's wrong will drive Everett crazy," he explained. "He wants to keep you safe. You matter to him. Give him a chance, and let him coddle you a bit. It'll make both of you feel better."

My stomach churned. No wonder Everett was concerned. He probably held himself responsible for what had happened to Danny. No doubt he believed he should have seen the signs, and now he was trying to make up for his perceived failure by being overprotective of me.

"I appreciate you telling me," I murmured. "I'll try to be more open. I actually don't mind his protectiveness." I loved it, in fact. "Thank you for sharing that with me."

He shrugged. "Be brave, and bear with him. He's worth it."

"I know." The words felt like acid in my throat. He was completely worth it, but would he think I was worth it when he discovered what his clan thought of me?

THIRTY-THREE

EVERETT

"We're practicing self-defense," I told Milo when we'd cleaned up after lunch. "Let's go to my place. There's a padded space in the garage we can use."

Milo nibbled his lower lip. He'd been looking at me differently since I'd come back from the bathroom. Danny must have said something about me, but I had no idea what. At least the curiosity in his expression had eased some of the upset he'd clearly been feeling earlier. Still, I needed to know what was bothering him so I could fix it. He'd been fine when we'd entered the shop and definitely not fine when we'd left.

"What happened while we were separated at the shop?" I asked during our walk from Dad and Momma's place back to mine. "Please, Milo. Tell me."

He didn't reply immediately, but I waited him out. Eventually, he heaved a sigh.

"Are you sure you're not disappointed I'm human?" he asked.

This again?

I took his hand. "Milo, I don't know how I can make it

any clearer. I adore you exactly as you are. You're perfect for me. The fates designed you that way."

"How am I perfect for you?" he asked quietly. "I can't shift, or run through the woods. I'm not as strong as you, or as brave. I'm just... not enough."

I stopped walking and spun him to face me. My eyes shifted as my bear fought to surface. "You are more than enough." I pulled him against my body and secured him there. "You're kind, and sweet, and smart. Those kids at the home already dote on you, and my family adores you. You *are* brave. You saw a man grow fangs and you threw hot sauce in his face and saved yourself. That's brave in my book."

He shook his head, his expression miserable. "But I needed you to rescue me."

"How do you know that?" I demanded. "Are you clairvoyant?"

"Of course not," he snapped. "But I was lost and would have starved or frozen if you hadn't saved me."

"You can't possibly know what would have happened," I argued. "Maybe you would have gotten out of the woods safely." I shook my head. "What brought this on?"

He cast his eyes down. "I overheard some shifters at the shop saying that it was wrong for you to be with me because I'm not one of you."

Fury coursed through me. I wanted to throw my head back and roar, then hunt down the bastards who'd made him feel inferior. He'd had enough of that in his life. He didn't need it from us. We were supposed to be his family, damn it.

"Listen carefully," I told him. "You are not lesser. You are not an outsider. You're exactly right in every way. I'll deal with those assholes later." I could already guess who he'd overheard. I'd seen John and his friend watching us as we'd entered the shop, and John was exactly the type of hateful person who'd say something like that.

"Please don't," Milo said. "I don't want to cause problems."

I smoothed his hair off his face and kissed his forehead. He closed his eyes and sagged against me.

"There won't be any problems," I assured him. But I *would* be having that talk. I tilted Milo's chin up and boosted him into my arms. He wrapped his legs around my waist and smiled shyly. I kissed him, wringing every ounce of passion from my soul so he'd be in no doubt of how much I craved him. "You're all I need," I murmured against his lips. "Just you."

He buried his face in the side of my neck and clung to me. Smiling, I continued along the path back to my place. Self-defense sounded even better now that everything was on the table. I wanted to give Milo the tools he needed to protect himself, but I wouldn't hate it if I got to have my hands all over him while doing it. Perhaps I'd even pin him down and torture him with my mouth. I whistled to myself. Yeah, that sounded promising.

THIRTY-FOUR

MILO

By the time Everett's improvised self-defense lesson ended, I was hornier than I'd ever been in my life. Being close to Everett, having his big body pin me down and his hands all over me—even in the most non-sexual of ways—really did it for me.

"Ev," I murmured as he helped me up. His eyes were gold, and his nostrils flared. Attraction sizzled between us where the palms of our hands touched. Holding hands had never felt so intimate.

"What do you need, Milo?" His voice was ragged, and as he spoke, his fangs slid into view. He was as affected by me as I was by him. I'd never dreamed such a thing was possible. How much of an idiot would I be to throw it away?

"I need you," I said. "Please mate me, Ev. Make me yours."

I felt empty. I ached to be filled, and I knew nothing but Everett's cock and the bond he'd spoken of would fix the sucking pit of need inside me.

He stiffened, his eyes searching mine. "Are you sure?

Mating isn't something you can change your mind about later. There's no need to rush."

"I want it," I insisted. "I might not fully understand how it works, but my soul feels like it's being torn, and I don't know how, but I know that mating is the only thing that will fix it. I want you bound to me forever. I won't regret it." If it meant Everett would spend the rest of his life looking at me the way he was now, I'd feel the opposite of regret. I had someone who adored me exactly for who I was. A man who was determined to give me the things I'd never had. How could I ever regret that? When Everett continued to hesitate, dread crept up on me. "But you don't have to if you don't want to." I forced myself to shrug. "It's okay."

It wasn't okay. It never would be. I needed him.

Everett swept me into his arms and cradled me across his chest. "Don't be crazy. You're my mate, and I never want you to doubt that again."

He carried me through the door that connected to the house and into his bedroom, where he gently lowered me onto the mattress.

"I won't break if you drop me," I said.

"My mate deserves better than that." He stared down at me, not moving and hardly blinking. "I want to memorize how you look right now, right before I claim you."

I shivered.

"Take off your clothes."

I hurried to tear off my socks and pants.

"Go easy," he said. "We have time."

I complied, even though I wanted to growl that I felt like I might burn up if I didn't get him inside me soon. For someone who'd never been a very sexual being, meeting Everett had brought out a side I didn't think I had. I lifted my shirt inch by inch, exposing more of my torso. He licked his lips and rumbled his approval. When I dropped the shirt, I was left in only my underwear. My erection thrust against the fabric, my cockhead soaked with precum, and my hole throbbed. The back of my underwear was wet with slick.

"Fuck, Milo, you're gorgeous." His eyes raked over me, and in that moment, I felt beautiful. I was no longer too short, too skinny, or unremarkable. In Everett's eyes, I was everything. I slid my hand down my body, tracing over my abdomen, and circled my cock. I stroked myself, my breath catching in the back of my throat as his eyes flashed gold, then brown, and his muscles tensed. I recognized the pose, and it inflamed me. Everett was a predator, ready to pounce.

I was his prey, and I reveled in it.

He yanked his shirt off, exposing his wide chest with that delicious dark hair I wanted to rub my face in. His arms flexed as he shoved his trousers down, and I imagined how wonderful they'd feel around me.

"You're so sexy," I breathed.

His briefs came off and then he stood at the foot of the bed, his thick cock an angry red and weeping. Precum was already smeared across his abs. His legs were solid and strong, reminding me of tree trunks. I wanted to climb him, wrap my legs around him, and hump him until we both came. But we could save that for another time.

"Tell me what to expect," I said, knowing I needed the details before we were too far gone.

"It's just like regular sex," he said, his eyes once again brown as they locked on mine. "Except that I'll bite you as I enter you and you'll feel a connection form between us. Then, when I come, I'll knot inside you."

"What's that mean?"

He grinned wolfishly. "When shifters come in their mates, our cocks swell and lock us inside them."

I frowned. I wasn't sure that sounded pleasant. "For how long?"

"Twenty minutes. Maybe half an hour." He shrugged. "That's just what I've heard. Obviously I can't say from personal experience because I've never come inside my mate before."

God, his eyes were hot. As were his words. I was so thankful both of us would be sharing a new experience. It made what was about to happen more meaningful.

"Well, you'd better change that," I teased.

He pounced on me, pinning me to the bed. Our slippery cocks rubbed against each other as his mouth met mine in a clash of lips, tongues, and teeth. He consumed me, taking over my attention so completely that I couldn't think of anything except getting more. My head fell back and he nipped my throat and sucked a bruise into the side of my neck, then another on my shoulder.

"This is where I'm going to bite you," he panted. "Then everyone will know you're mine."

"Fuck, yeah." I worked my hips, loving the exquisite glide of our cocks and the friction of his hair against my sensitive skin.

Everett gave my cock a lazy tug. I keened and thrust, seeking more, but he released me and pushed his blunt fingers between my cheeks instead. He probed at my hole, and slipped the tip of a finger inside. There was no burn since I was already loose and turned on, but the fullness wasn't enough. I needed more. When he pushed it in up to the knuckle, I cried out. Then he stroked my prostate and my vision went fuzzy.

My head lolled back and I was vaguely aware of him adding a second finger, then a third. He gave me slow, drugging kisses that smothered my sounds of pleasure. When he withdrew his hand, I whimpered at the loss.

Everett's face appeared above me, his eyes golden fire. "Are you sure?"

"Yes," I panted.

He didn't ask again. Instead, he notched his massive cock at my entrance and rocked inside inch by inch. My mouth fell open. I was so full of him, it felt as if we were becoming one. My dick jerked between us, spilling precum.

Everett lowered his mouth to my shoulder. I forced myself to relax when I felt his fangs, but I couldn't help shouting as they pierced the skin. They sunk deep, and pain lanced through me, but it didn't make me want to shove him off. Instead, I clutched him closer and felt his presence wrap around me like a blanket.

I had a vague sense of his emotions. Satisfaction, wonder, and a joy so deep it made tears prickle at the backs of my eyes. I felt him at the edge of my mind, probing my own emotions. It was as if we were yin and yang, wrapped inexorably around each other. His teeth retracted and he licked the wound.

"You okay?" he asked hoarsely.

"Perfect." My voice was dreamy, and I felt as though I was floating through space. My erection had flagged, but he wrapped his hand around it and coaxed it back to life. Then he was moving inside me, lighting me up. Images and thoughts flashed through my mind, but I wasn't sure if they were his or mine.

Beautiful.

Perfect.

Ours.

Mate.

I mentally reached out and realized it was his bear

communicating with me. Love swelled in my chest and I let him feel it.

"Milo," Everett murmured. "Mate."

Pressure zapped down my spine. My dick throbbed in his grasp.

"Oh Gods, I'm going to come."

"Yes," he growled, pounding into me with an almost feral energy. "Give me your come, little mate."

"Uhn!" I released all over his hand, shuddering and chanting his name.

He grunted and his cock thickened inside of me, pressing against my prostate and swelling until I knew there was no way we could be separated. This must be the knot he'd talked about. It felt incredible, locking us together. Making us one.

"Milo," he ground out, his teeth fastening onto my shoulder again, not breaking the skin, just resting there. "My mate."

Carefully, he rolled us onto our sides and cradled me in his arms. With his knot still inside me and the wound on my shoulder throbbing, a sense of deep contentment washed over me. I'd never felt more like I belonged.

THIRTY-FIVE

EVERETT

Having a mate was awesome. I couldn't believe how connected I felt to Milo. I'd been aching for him since we'd met, but now it was as though every fiber of my being was attuned to him. If he entered the room, I knew it. If he moved nearby, goosebumps rippled over my skin, and when he walked up behind me while I was cooking our steak for dinner and pressed a kiss on the bare skin between my shoulder blades, I was immediately hard. His scent danced around me, cherries and vanilla, a little tart and a lot sweet. My dick pressed against the fly of my jeans and I gritted my teeth, regretting that I hadn't put underwear on.

"Ev," he murmured, his breath whispering over my skin. "Mate."

My teeth bared in a feral smile I was grateful he couldn't see. "Mate," I agreed.

My dick throbbed again. My instincts screamed at me to turn around and bury myself in him, especially when I could smell that he was as aroused as me, but I resisted. Not only was it his first time taking my knot, but he'd been a virgin. His ass needed a break.

His slender arms wrapped around my middle and his cheek rested on my back.

"You're making it hard to focus," I growled.

"I don't care if you burn it."

My lips twisted into a smug smile. Milo wanted me even more than he wanted good food, and I'd learned that food was very important to him.

"What about the salad you were supposed to be making?" I asked.

"It's ready to go, and the breadsticks are in the oven."

"Oh." I must have been too consumed by his scent and the sounds he made to have noticed him finishing.

His fingers splayed over my abs and played with my belly hair. "I love this."

I covered one of his hands with my own and pushed it lower, over the bulge at the front of my jeans. His breath caught.

"I want you," he whispered.

"Not yet, baby." I guided his hand, rubbing it over the bulge, and my eyes rolled back in my head. "After dinner, I'll suck your pretty cock dry."

Milo whined in protest and continued petting my dick. "I want you to fuck me."

"You're too sore," I told him. "We can do that again tomorrow."

"Promise?"

"I promise." I turned to kiss him, brushing my lips over his kiss-swollen ones. The sight of his cheeks, still pink from beard burn, sent a rush of possessiveness through me and I kissed him again. I nuzzled the puncture marks on his shoulder. I'd licked them earlier, so they hadn't bled too much—shifter saliva contained a natural coagulant—but it would take a while for them to heal, especially since he was human. "Everyone is going to know you're mine as soon as they see your mark."

His eyes shone with joy. I kissed him once more and returned my attention to the steak. No matter how much I indulged my possessive side, I doubted it would be too much for Milo. After a lifetime of feeling unwanted and unloved, he visibly lit up any time I called him mine. He wanted someone to belong to and with, and that someone was me.

A knock sounded on the front door.

"Are you expecting anyone?" I asked Milo. "Because I'm not."

"No." He let me go and came around to my side. "Should I get it?"

"No, you stay here." Where I'd be able to protect him. My gaze skimmed down his body. "Perhaps you could put a shirt on though? If it's one of my nosy family members, I don't want them seeing your gorgeous body."

"Okay." He smiled happily and headed toward the bedrooms. Meanwhile, I took the steak off the heat and went to the front door. My family could stare at my naked chest all they liked.

Zander stood on the doorstep and judging by his expression, it wasn't a social call.

"What's up?" I asked, inviting him in.

His eyes narrowed as soon as he stepped inside and he looked at me appraisingly. I smirked. He could probably smell the spunk on me. Either that or the scent of sex lingered in the air. Zander's sense of smell was even more sensitive than mine.

"You and Milo?" he asked.

Milo darted into the hall, coming to a stop when he saw Zander. He slunk to my side, perhaps sensing the same thing I did—that Zander was here on serious business. My brother's eyes did a quick dip to Milo's shoulder and his nostrils flared. The mate mark was hidden from sight, but it was possible he could detect the faint metallic scent of blood.

I kissed Milo's cheek. "Milo and I are mated."

Zander's craggy face broke into a smile. "Congratulations, brother. And Milo," he turned his attention to my mate, who squirmed. "Welcome to the family."

"Thank you," Milo said.

"Appreciate it, Z." I tilted my head toward the end of the hall. "We're cooking dinner. Why don't you come in and tell us whatever you need to?"

In the kitchen, I returned the steak to the heat and poured a drink for each of us. We sat around at the breakfast bar, which matched the one in my parents' house.

Zander sipped his water—he was still on duty—and sighed. "Clay saw a wolf near our parents' place an hour ago."

I tensed. "Did he follow it?"

"For as long as he could, but the wolf was faster than him and lost him in the woods."

"Damn." My fingers clenched around my glass. "Was it Tomas?"

Zander pulled a face. "Hard to say. The description fits the previous sighting, but we don't have a lot of information to work with."

Worry and fear pulsed through the mate bond and I reached for Milo's hand. "It's all right, baby," I soothed. "He won't get to you."

"But what if he hurts someone else?" Milo asked quietly.

"It's unlikely he will," Zander answered, saving me the

trouble. "He's fixated on you. You're the only one he's interested in."

I felt Milo's helplessness like a physical punch to the gut.

"If he comes for Milo, I will do whatever it takes to keep my mate safe," I said to Zander, knowing he'd read my intention. "*Whatever* it takes."

His eyes flashed. "We don't want a war with the rogue pack."

My bear growled. He didn't give a shit who we went to war with as long as Milo was safe.

Zander raised an eyebrow. "I'm trying to set up a meeting with the pack's Alpha, but he isn't cooperating."

"Doesn't that tell you all you need to know?" If they wouldn't help us, then they were condoning the wolf's behavior. That couldn't stand.

Zander gave me a cut-the-bullshit look and pushed his chair back. "I have to get back to the office. Ev, if the wolf comes after your man, you do what you've got to do, but keep in mind what's best for the town."

I nodded. I got his point, but he had no idea what it was like to have a mate or he wouldn't ask me to exercise judgment. When it came to Milo, I had no restraint.

Zander saw himself out.

I patted my lap and Milo sat. I cradled him in my arms and murmured soft reassurances that I wouldn't let anything happen to him. Once we'd both calmed, we ate our dinner, I made good on my promise to suck Milo's brains out through his cock, and then I bundled him in blankets in front of the TV and put on a romantic comedy. I fell asleep with him in my arms.

CHAPTER

THIRTY-SIX

MILO

I woke with my head on Everett's chest. My neck hurt from being cramped on the sofa while we slept, but even the twinge of pain couldn't remove the joy I felt at being mated to Everett. No one else would ever know the blissful sensation of sleeping in Everett's arms. That honor was reserved for me. No one else would experience his kisses or discover how masterful he was at making love. This big, gruff bear was all mine.

I smiled to myself, feeling giddy. Even the throb of my shoulder didn't bother me. It simply reminded me that Everett had claimed me and in the eyes of the shifter community, I was his and he was mine. I'd felt the force of his emotions pouring through the bond yesterday. The strength of his adoration and wonder had brought tears to my eyes. No one else had ever seen me the way he did, and they never would.

But as for what else being mated meant... I didn't know.

I supposed I'd be moving to Grizzly Ridge, so presumably I'd have to quit my job. I had mixed feelings about that. I'd give up anything for Everett, but I'd fought with everything I had to get through college and land a stable job I could rely on. Could I take such a leap of faith? And if I were to resign, was I supposed to move in with Everett, or would he want me to live somewhere else?

"You're thinking awfully hard," Everett rumbled.

I snuggled closer to him. "Just wondering about what comes next."

"With the wolf?" he asked sleepily.

"With us," I corrected. "Like... it's occurred to me that maybe I don't fully understand what mating means for my life."

Everett stiffened. "Are you having regrets?"

He sounded fully awake now.

"No!" I exclaimed, horrified he'd think that. "I've never been this happy. But with human relationships, I know how things are supposed to progress, even if I haven't technically been in one. With us, I'm a bit lost." He nibbled his lower lip. "I guess I'm moving to Grizzly Ridge?"

Everett's big body relaxed and he kissed my cheek. "It depends on what you're comfortable with, but yes, I'd love it if you moved to Grizzly Ridge."

"With you?" I asked.

"Look at me."

I rolled to face him, gazing into his gorgeous dark eyes and finding all the reassurance I could possibly want reflecting back at me.

"I know this might be fast by human standards, but I would like nothing more than for you to move in with me."

My heart soared. I was wanted. Needed. An invisible presence wrapped around me, cocooning me with warmth. "But I can't do my job from here."

I was a junior accountant. Easily replaceable. They'd never grant me permission to work remotely.

He searched my eyes. "Do you love your job?"

"No." The word popped out of my mouth without conscious thought. "But I love the stability it brings me."

His face softened and he drew me into a sweet kiss. "If you want to stay in Grayton until you've found a stable job here, then I'll come with you. I understand why you'd want that." He hesitated, then added, "But if you're open to the idea, I earn enough to provide for both of us. You could resign and let me take care of everything until you find a job that lights you up every day."

Nerves and excitement circled my gut, present in equal measure. My instincts urged me to say yes and work out the details later, but that little voice of fear in the back of my mind asked if I was crazy. I'd fought for financial safety. If I gave it up to be with Everett, then I'd lose everything if we didn't work out.

You're mated, I reminded myself. *There is no "it won't work out."*

But that was still difficult for me to get my head around. I was used to human relationships, and a high percentage of marriages ended in divorce. Was I willing to risk everything?

"Milo?" Everett prompted.

"I don't know," I said helplessly. "What if I'm a burden? What if we fight? What if you decide you don't want me?"

"You won't be." To his credit, Everett's tone and expression were deadly serious. "It would be my honor to support you while you chase your dream."

"But I don't know what that is!"

He smiled. "We can figure it out together."

Everything inside me pulled tight. I felt like a rubber band stretched nearly to the breaking point. Something had to give. But then that lovely sense of warmth eased through me again, loosening my muscles and relieving the tension. It was so right. In that instant, I knew. If I took a leap of faith to be with Everett, every day could be like this, surrounded by comfort and love.

"Okay." The single word seemed to boom in my head. I was really doing this. Me, the king of not trying new things. "I'd like to quit my job and move in with you."

Everett beamed wider than I'd ever seen him smile before. "I promise you won't regret it."

The nerves in my gut fell away, leaving only the excitement. I snuggled against his chest.

"I'm going to email my resignation later today."

The warmth inside me expanded, and my lips curved as I listened to the rhythmic thump of Everett's heart. Now that I'd made the decision, I wished I didn't have to return to work at all, but I doubted I could get away with that. Not even for the sake of love.

THIRTY-SEVEN

EVERETT

I served Milo breakfast in bed and then we made love. When we emerged from a sex haze, it was nearly lunchtime, so we walked to the bakery together.

"Do you feel like something savory or sweet?" I asked him as we entered.

"Savory, I think." He winked at me. "We don't all have your sweet tooth."

I chuckled, feeling more at ease than I could ever remember being before despite the knowledge that the wolf might be watching us. Let him watch. Maybe he'd see that Milo had been mated and give up. I doubted it, but stranger things had happened, and I was too busy enjoying the way his small hand fit in mine to let anything ruin the mood.

Milo ordered a scone and I asked for a cinnamon roll and a slice of cake, along with a hot drink for each of us, and paid. We sat in the corner and waited for the food to be brought over. We chatted while we ate. I regaled Milo with tales of growing up in Grizzly Ridge and he opened up to me more about his past in foster care. I was relieved to hear it hadn't all been bad, and that he'd had pockets of happiness over the years.

When we'd finished eating, we ordered another round of coffee, enjoying ourselves too much to end the date. Skye, the female omega who'd served us, brought the drinks over.

"I hear congratulations are in order," she said, eyeing Milo's shoulder.

"They are." I reached across the table and took Milo's hand. "Milo is my mate. Milo, let me properly introduce Skye. She's a bear shifter, like me."

Milo's hand tightened around mine, but he smiled at Skye. "It's nice to meet you."

"You too." Her smile reached her eyes, and I knew Milo had noticed that too because his grip relaxed. "I'm so pleased that Everett has found his mate."

An idea struck. "Skye, why don't you join us for a moment?" I asked. "Nobody is waiting to be served."

She glanced around, then sat. "Only for five minutes." She gave Milo her full attention. "Momma Melinda told me you do something fancy in the city."

Milo laughed, but I didn't hear his reply, too distracted by Danny, who'd appeared behind the counter and was waving me over. I hesitated, reluctant to leave Milo alone. He caught my eye and gave me a slight nod. Grateful, I headed over to my brother.

"What is it?" I asked as I drew near.

He motioned for me to follow him to the corner farthest from Milo and Skye, then waited for me to take the chair facing me—as he knew I would, the smug bastard.

"There's something I need to say to you." Danny sat to the side, so he wasn't obscuring my view of my mate.

My brow furrowed. "Is everything okay?"

He waved his hand back and forth in a so-so gesture.

"Um." He cleared his throat. "Okay, I don't know the best way to do this, so I'm just going to get straight to the point."

"All right." Worry crept over me.

"I've noticed that you're hyper-aware of Milo's safety, and I'm guessing it's because of me."

I pursed my lips. "He's my mate. Of course I'm protective."

He smiled. "I don't doubt that, but what I'm saying is that maybe you're a bit more attuned to what's going on with him because of what happened between Rex and me."

I gritted my teeth. Rex was his abusive asshole of an ex-boyfriend. I didn't reply, because I couldn't deny it. I'd over-looked the fact Danny was in trouble when it was right under my nose. Of course I was keeping a close eye on Milo so I didn't repeat that mistake.

"I'm sorry that my bad decisions have made you feel like you always have to be on guard," Danny said.

My jaw dropped. "What the fuck? Your bad decisions? Like hell. Something was wrong, and I should have noticed. That's on me."

Danny folded his arms across his chest. "I intentionally hid it from you. How were you supposed to know? Can you read minds?"

"I should have seen the signs." God knew they'd been there, even if I'd only noticed them in hindsight.

"I didn't want you to know." Danny's tone was softer now. "So you didn't."

My throat constricted. "But why?"

It was the question that had plagued me. Why hadn't my sweet omega brother felt like he could come to me for help?

Danny's delicate features twisted through a range of

expressions before settling on one I couldn't read. "Because I was ashamed."

I glanced at Milo and Skye, but they weren't paying us any attention. "You had no reason to be."

He sighed. "You, Zander, and Garrick wouldn't have let yourselves get into a situation like that. I thought the fact I had was yet more proof that I was the weakest brother, and I didn't want you to see me that way."

I could hardly believe my ears. "It's different. Like it or not, alphas have advantages that omegas don't. We're stronger, bigger, and we heal faster. If one of us had pushed back against an abusive boyfriend, the consequences would've been far less severe than they could have been for you. He could have killed you."

"But he didn't," Danny said. "So you can stop using me as an excuse to go into overprotective alpha bear mode. I'm okay, and Milo will be too."

"It's not an excuse. I let you down."

"And I let you down too." Danny yanked me into a hug. "You have nothing to be sorry for."

I hugged him back fiercely. "Neither do you."

THIRTY-EIGHT

MILO

I rolled the bread dough out and cut it into individual portions, then placed them on a tray and handed them to Danny to put in the oven. It was Monday, Danny's day off, and he and Melinda had managed to convince Everett to go to work since both of them had promised to stay with me at all times.

Danny opened the oven and hot air wafted out, carrying the scent of cooking bacon and egg pastries. My stomach churned. I'd been feeling off all day.

"Mmm, smell that," Danny said. "Good, right?"

I clapped a hand to my mouth as bile rose up the back of my throat. I raced to the bathroom and dropped to my knees in front of the toilet just in time to throw up my breakfast. My stomach clenched and heaved, emptying out every last bit, and I panted as the retching finally subsided.

"Here."

A water bottle appeared beside me. I took it gratefully and rinsed the bitter taste out of my mouth.

"Sorry, I think I might be getting a tummy bug." I tried to get up.

Danny grabbed my arm and steadied me as my head swam. "You need to sit down. Come on."

He led me to the living room. I sat on the sofa and pulled my knees up to my chest, shielding my sensitive stomach.

"Have you been feeling sick all day?" Melinda asked as she entered. She offered me a strawberry candy to suck on, and I took it, relieved when my stomach didn't revolt.

"A little unsettled," I admitted. "But I thought I was making a fuss out of nothing. Sorry, I should never have touched the food for the kids. You'll have to re-do it now."

"Maybe." Melinda dragged a chair over to sit opposite me. Her expression was thoughtful. "Or it could be something else."

She and Danny exchanged a look.

"What?" I demanded. I was the one with the upset tummy, after all.

"Is it possible you could be pregnant?" Melinda asked.

"W-What?" I stared at them blankly.

She gave me a Mona Lisa smile. "Do you use blockers, Milo? Did you and Everett use protection when you mated?"

Ugh. I could go for the rest of my life without hearing those words come out of her mouth again. I didn't want to think about motherly Melinda and sex at the same time. Then the meaning of her words sank in.

"I didn't know Everett could get me pregnant. I'm a human. He's a shifter. Is that even possible?"

Danny shrugged. "We haven't seen it here in Grizzly Ridge before, but that doesn't mean it's not possible."

"Especially as there's always the possibility you have latent shifter DNA," Melinda added. "Just because it doesn't manifest itself doesn't mean it's not there."

"Oh, Gods." Could I be pregnant? I'd never in a million

years considered having a baby, although when I thought about what it would be like to raise one with Everett, I liked the idea. He'd be a wonderful father. The kind I'd always dreamed of having. But wouldn't having me as the other dad screw the kid up? How could I possibly be a good dad when I didn't know what that was supposed to look like?

"Hang on a second," I said. "Even if it were possible, it was only a few days ago that we mated. I wouldn't be having symptoms already."

Melinda and Danny exchanged another glance.

"The timing of shifter pregnancies isn't the same as for humans," Melinda said. "The early stages are accelerated, and the gestation period is shorter." She stood, and offered me a hand. "There's only one way to know for sure. Let's go to the pharmacy and get a test."

I took her hand and let her lead me out of the house, the food for the children temporarily forgotten.

"Should I stay to keep an eye on the oven?" Danny asked.

Melinda pursed her lips. "You'd better come. Ev would lose his mind if he found out we let Milo leave with only one of us for protection. We won't be long."

I wordlessly got into the car, but my mind was racing. Everett and I had never discussed kids. What if I was pregnant and he got upset? I'd only just found him. I didn't want to lose him again.

"It's going to be okay," Danny said, patting my arm.

Melinda parked outside the pharmacy and we went in as a group. She stopped in front of the shelves that displayed pregnancy tests and scanned the options.

"This will do," she said, choosing one. She hesitated, then grabbed a different box as well. "Can't be too careful."

We made our way to the register, and it finally struck me that this was a small town and the three of us buying pregnancy tests would have the locals buzzing with gossip in no time. Hopefully it didn't get back to Everett before I was able to tell him. Perhaps I could get Melinda to stop by his work on the way home. Melinda paid for the boxes, then tucked them into her handbag, which she passed to me.

"I'm going to order a coffee from the bakery," she said. "While I'm waiting, you can use their restroom to do the test. That way, we can tell Everett before he finds out from anyone else."

"Good thinking."

The bakery was next door. Danny ushered us in, grumbling about having to visit work on his day off, but I could tell he was just teasing. While he and Melinda approached the counter, I hurried to the restroom. I peed on both sticks and lined them up on the sink, then set my phone timer for two minutes. One line appeared. Tension knotted inside of me. I stared at the tests, hard, and nearly forgot to breathe when a second line began to appear.

Beside the sink, the translucent glass window suddenly shattered inward. I gasped and stumbled back to avoid flying shards of glass. I blinked, trying to make sense of what I was seeing. A man appeared in the window frame.

Tomas.

Only his eyes shone a sickly yellow-green and fangs protruded from between his lips. He lunged through the window and grabbed me. I tried to shove him away, but he was too strong. He hauled me toward the window and jumped through, dragging me behind him like a sack of potatoes. Glass scored my skin, and I screamed.

"Help!" I shouted, hoping that any shifters in the area would hear, even if a normal human couldn't. "Help!"

Tomas clapped his hand over my mouth. He nodded to another man, who opened the trunk of a waiting car. Tomas lifted me off my feet.

"Everett!" I yelled. "I need you!"

There was a crash in the restroom and then Danny was on the other side of the window. I locked eyes with him and reached out, knowing there was no way he'd be able to get to me but still holding out hope.

Tomas tossed me in the trunk. My back crunched as it hit the hard surface and I struggled for breath, the impact having driven the air from my lungs. A ringing sound shrilled in my ears. The trunk slammed shut and a few seconds later, the car started moving.

THIRTY-NINE

EVERETT

High-schoolers thought they knew everything. A sea of bored faces stared back at me as I tried to explain the role of the Search and Rescue team to the Grizzly Ridge junior class. They got us to do this each year in the hopes we'd either find new recruits or at least impress on the next generation the importance of what we did. I was halfway through a story from one of our rescues when a wave of fear more intense than anything I'd ever experienced slammed into me. I staggered backward, my hand going automatically to my shoulder. It tingled in the same place I'd left Milo's mating bite.

Terror rushed through me. Something was wrong with Milo. Something bad. He was scared out of his mind.

"I have to go." I raised my hand in a distracted farewell as I bolted from the room. The instant I was outside, I took my phone from my pocket and called Danny. "Milo."

"He's been taken." Danny's words sent a chill down my spine. "We're at the bakery. They snatched him out of the restroom."

"I'm on my way. Call Zander."

I hung up and ran to my car. The drive to the bakery only took a few minutes, but it felt like eons. When I pulled up out front, Zander was already there.

"Clay and Azizi are searching for the car," Zander said as I crossed the space between us. "Danny got the license plate before they drove away."

"Thank fuck. At least that's something."

He nodded. "We have a BOLO out and any sightings will be reported to Clay. We're working on the assumption that they're heading back to Moonlight Cove."

"What can I do?" I asked, mentally cursing myself for leaving Milo today. The high-schoolers could have waited, and we hadn't had any other important calls. I should have stayed with him, no matter what Momma and Danny said.

Zander rubbed his jaw. "Are you able to sense anything about Milo's whereabouts through the mate bond?"

"I sensed fear when he was taken." I still felt cold inside, and that was only from experiencing it secondhand. I closed my eyes and focused on the bond connecting me to Milo. I sent energy out along it, searching for him, but I didn't encounter anything. Not even remnants of fear from earlier. "There's nothing now," I said, feeling sick at what that might mean. "He might be unconscious."

"Shit." Zander waved toward the bakery door. "Go in. Talk to Momma and Danny. I already have, but you might pick up something I missed."

I strode inside, relieved to have a purpose, even if it wasn't hunting down Milo the way I'd like to. Unfortunately, I wouldn't be able to follow his scent because they'd escaped in a vehicle, and with him being scarily absent from the bond, I couldn't sense proximity either. I was useless.

"Ev!" Danny rushed at me, his eyes wide and apologetic. "I'm so sorry. We thought he'd be safe in the restroom. We were out here, so no one could go past without us seeing, but we didn't think about the window."

My jaw tightened. I wanted to rage that their thoughtlessness could cost Milo everything, but that wouldn't help. I hauled in a deep breath and willed my bear to calm down.

Find mate, he insisted. *Kill enemy.*

Yeah. Later. All the killer instinct in the world wouldn't do much good if I didn't know where Milo was.

"Why did you leave the house?" I demanded. "I thought you were going to stay there, other than to run the food to the children's home."

Danny bit his lip and looked down. There was something he wasn't telling me.

"What is it?" My temper soared. "My mate is in danger. I need to know."

"Milo was queasy." Momma's hand landed on my forearm and I flinched. I'd been so absorbed in Danny that I hadn't noticed her approach. "We took him to the pharmacy."

"Then why were you here? You could have just gone there and returned home immediately."

She nodded. "We probably should have, but we wanted answers so we could make sure you heard the truth before any rumors got around."

I frowned. "Rumors?" She was speaking in riddles, and it drove me insane. "What's your point?"

She handed me a long, thin object. I took it and stared down blankly, my brain struggling to register what I was seeing because it was so out of context. Finally, it was as if my vision cleared and a terrifying truth settled in my chest.

It was a positive pregnancy test.

Milo was pregnant.

He wasn't the only one in danger. Our cub's life was on the line too. I threw my head back and roared. My bear ripped to the surface and I bounded through the exit and onto the street. My mate and my cub were under threat, and it was all my fault.

CHAPTER

FORTY

MILO
I peered around the dimly lit space, hoping to see something I could use to figure out where I was. My eyes had adjusted as much as they were going to, and I could make out boxes stacked against the opposite wall and gym equipment in the center of the floor. Based on the stairs descending from the door to the ground, it might be someone's basement. I turned to look at my wrists, which were chained to a metal pipe. My head throbbed from the movement. I'd made too much noise on the way here, so they'd stopped the car just long enough to knock me out. When I'd woken, I'd already been in chains.

The dirty ground was cold beneath me, leaching the warmth from my body. I looked around, searching for something I could use as a buffer between myself and the dirt, but everything had been moved out of reach. Two men argued upstairs, but between my pounding headache and the muffling effect of the door, I couldn't tell what they were saying. Whatever it was, they clearly disagreed with each other. I could only hope the one who wasn't Tomas objected to keeping a prisoner chained in the basement.

A door slammed, and the voices stopped. I stayed quiet, praying that Tomas had been the one to leave, but my prayers were thwarted when a key sounded in the lock at the top of the stairs and the door swung inward to reveal the man of my nightmares. He stomped down the stairs toward me, and I instinctively backed up, but I hit the wall and couldn't go any further. There was nowhere to hide.

Tomas's clothes didn't look as if they'd been washed recently—a fact I'd been too scared to notice earlier—and his eyes glowed that eerie yellow-green. His wolf had taken over control. He stopped a few paces from me, and my stomach lurched when his scent reached my nostrils. He smelled of stale body odor. My stomach rolled and complained.

Don't, I warned it.

He stepped closer, and I emptied the pitiful contents of my gut onto the ground in front of his shoes.

"Disgusting," he growled. When I glanced up, his nostrils were flared and his lip curled in scorn. "What did I do to deserve a pathetic mate like you?"

I shook my head, and my eyes watered. Damn. I needed to remember to stop moving. "I'm not your mate."

He laughed, the sound humorless. "Of course you are. You shouldn't have run from me. You've only made things worse for yourself."

"I can't be your mate," I protested, hoping he'd see reason. "I already have a mate."

"No." He seized my collar and dragged me to my feet. "You don't have a mate mark. I checked when you arrived for our date." He shoved back the fabric of my shirt and froze. A muscle in the corner of his jaw ticked, and then, before I had time to brace myself, he backhanded me across the face. Stars exploded in front of my eyes and I tasted blood. I reeled, hitting the wall and sinking as far as the chains would allow. My head screamed with agony, and all I could think of was the baby I'd just discovered. What if Tomas did something to hurt them?

I couldn't antagonize him any more than I already had. I needed to play it smart.

"You disgusting whore," he snapped, kicking my feet out from under me. The chains cut into my wrists as they suddenly took on more of my weight. I staggered to my feet, blood trickling down my forearm.

Don't look. Don't look.

If I saw it, I'd faint, and then there was no telling what he'd do.

Tomas leaned close, his foul breath making my stomach heave. "The bear who gave you that mark is a false mate. He can't be your fated mate, because *I* am. I knew it the instant I smelled you." He gave me a sinister smile. "Don't worry. When I bite you, the bear's mark will fade. Our bond will replace the false bond."

A cold finger slithered down my spine. Was that true? Could Tomas destroy my bond with Everett? I could endure anything if I knew that Everett would come for me, but without the bond, I might lose everything I'd come to treasure. I loved him. I knew it was fast, and that most people would think it was crazy, but I loved Everett with every beat of my heart and the thought of being cut off from him was physically painful.

Tomas cupped my face. "I can see your hope. You're an open book to me. You think your bear will come for you, but he won't. He won't bother saving a false mate. Especially not a weak human who doesn't have a place in his clan."

My heart fell. It was as if he'd peeked into my mind and witnessed my deepest fears.

No, I told myself. *Don't believe it. Everett will come.*

Please, let him come.

CHAPTER

FORTY-ONE

VERETT

Zander and I entered the police station and the receptionist raised a hand to get our attention.

"What is it?" Zander asked sharply.

She didn't flinch. "The Alpha of the rogue wolf pack called," she said. "He left you a message."

I sucked in a breath. "What did he say?"

She glanced at me, then back to Zander. "Sir?"

He nodded. "Go ahead."

"He said that the pack has banished Tomas. They don't condone a shifter taking another shifter's mate, and he hopes there are no hard feelings."

"No hard feelings?" I repeated, stunned. How could there be no hard feelings? They'd brought Tomas into the area and he'd endangered Milo. Although... I supposed if not for him, I might not have met my mate.

"He also said," she lowered her voice, "that they'll leave him to your mercy."

I rolled my eyes. "For fuck's sake. That's just their way of avoiding a war without actually having to do anything useful." What a coward.

"Calm down," Zander said. I shot him a glare. He raised an eyebrow. "Getting angry at the pack won't serve any purpose. What's important is figuring out how to get Milo back." He turned to the receptionist. "Did he say where Tomas is?"

"No, sir."

"See?" I prompted. "Useless."

"Not helpful." Zander headed for the open-plan area where his officers' desks were housed. He cleared off the table in the center, grabbed the map of the region from the wall, and sat.

"Have you heard from Clay?" I asked.

"Nothing worth mentioning." He grabbed a pen and traced a line between Grizzly Ridge and Moonlight Cove. "If you were a banished wolf, possibly on the verge of turning feral, where would you hide?"

"I'd go somewhere familiar," I said. "Probably closer to Moonlight Cove since the risk of someone reporting me would be lower. Everyone around here is on alert, and he probably knows that."

"You don't think he'd have taken Milo out of state?"

I scratched my chin. "I doubt it. From what Danny said, Milo was in the trunk of the car. He couldn't stay there indefinitely. They'd have to get him out, and that would be easier to do in a controlled environment." A bitter taste flooded my mouth at the thought of Milo locked in a strange place with the wolf he was terrified of. He must feel so alone. I should never have stopped watching him. I'd let him down, just like I had let Danny down.

Voices sounded in the hall and two police officers I didn't recognize—they must have come from a nearby township—entered, along with the rest of the Search and Rescue Team. They all wore uniforms, and there wasn't a smiling face among the group. Yuri slung an arm around my shoulder.

"It's okay, Ev," he said gruffly. "We'll get your man back."

"Thanks for coming." My throat thickened with emotion. I didn't know why I was so touched. Finding people was literally our job—even if it wasn't usually in these circumstances—but I'd never been so personally invested before. I couldn't put my emotions to the side while we got to the bottom of this. My love for Milo was all-consuming. There was no compartmentalizing it.

Behind the crew, a pair of broad shoulders filled the door. Dad nodded to me and gestured for me to join him. I pulled free of Yuri's hold and strode over.

"We'll find him," he said, clasping my shoulder with a steady grip. "Your mother won't let her newest son go that easily."

I rubbed my lips together and tried to think stoic thoughts. I would not cry at how perfect it sounded to hear him refer to Milo as a son. "Thanks, Dad."

He watched me carefully, and I sensed he had something else to say. When he spoke, he took me by surprise. "I understand wanting to be involved in the rescue operation, but you should let Zander lead the charge. You won't be as clear-headed as you usually are."

I frowned at him. "If Momma was in danger, would you let someone else lead the charge?"

His expression became wry. "No. But I had to say it."

"And now you have." I would ignore him. I knew his suggestion had come from a good place, and it was probably solid advice, but there was no way in hell I was leaving Milo's welfare in someone else's hands. Not even my brother's.

"Come on." I jerked a thumb at the table. "We don't want to be left out of the plan."

CHAPTER

FORTY-TWO

MILO
My arms screamed for relief. Every muscle throbbed, and as I shifted, trying to ease the pain, a cramp locked up my shoulder. My breath caught and tears stung my eyes.

It will be okay.

My cheek burned where Tomas had hit me, but at least he hadn't been back since then. I wasn't sure how much time had passed. It could have been minutes or hours. Probably at least an hour, judging by the strain in my muscles. My stomach clenched, but it was too empty for me to be sick. At least there were some upsides to my predicament.

The cramp passed and I slumped, remembering at the last minute not to put too much weight on my bound wrist in case I yanked the joint out of the socket. A floorboard creaked upstairs and I froze. It sounded close. My gaze flew to the door. The handle started to turn, and then it eased inward.

Oh, Gods.

My head spun, and I focused on peering through the sudden light at the figure who appeared at the top of the stairs, hoping I wouldn't pass out if I could remain firmly grounded in the present. Before the guy was even halfway down the stairs, I could tell it wasn't Tomas. This man was bigger. His dark hair was tied at the nape of his neck, and his face was covered in stubble. His lips were full and firm, his eyes unsmiling. I gulped. Whoever he was, he didn't look friendly.

The man stomped across the floor and stopped just out of reach. He crossed his arms over his burly chest and stared at me as though I were an insect under a magnifying glass. I waited for him to say something, but the moment dragged on in silence. I took advantage of the opportunity to study him back.

I had no idea if he was human, or something else. Based on the fact Tomas was a wolf and everyone around here seemed to have an alter ego, I could assume he wasn't completely human. He was as large as some of the men from Grizzly Ridge, but I had no idea if shifter type correlated to size. Maybe it just meant he was a powerful alpha.

He rolled his leather jacket-clad shoulders and inhaled deeply. A strange look came across his face. He moved closer, his eyes dipping to where my mating mark lay beneath my shirt.

"I'm going to look at your mark." His voice was a deep rumble, almost a growl. It didn't sound as though he spoke often.

"Okay." It wasn't as if I could fight him anyway. At least he'd given me a heads-up before putting his hands on me.

He dragged my collar aside and studied the mark, then nodded to himself, as if he'd confirmed something. But then, quick as a flash, his eyes changed and his fangs dropped. His eyes were green, like Tomas's, but without the feral yellow glow. He sucked in a breath, his nostrils flaring, and his tongue darted out to wet his lips.

"You smell good."

Ah, fuck. I stared at him in disbelief. Was I about to have another shifter declare himself my mate? What was in the water around here?

He leaned closer and sniffed the junction of my neck and shoulder. I tried not to tremble. It would be so easy for him to tear my throat out with those teeth. But then he shook his head.

"It's not you." He circled me, still sniffing. "You smell of my mate. You've been in contact with them. Fuck." He dragged a hand down his rugged face and stepped back. "What the hell am I going to do with you?"

"Set me free?" I suggested, very optimistically. I might have been in contact with his mate, but they could be anyone. It certainly didn't mean this guy—whatever he was—was suddenly on my side.

"This was supposed to be easy money," he grumbled. "All I had to do was drive the damn car. He told me you were mated, but that you had a mental disorder and he needed help to get you home." He scanned the chains and cuffs with disgust. "This isn't how anyone treats their mate, and that bite on your shoulder is from a bear, not a wolf." He kicked one of the boxes lining the opposite wall. "This is just my goddamn luck."

"I don't have a mental disorder, and I'm not his mate," I said, in case he had any lingering doubt. "I'm perfectly sane, and I don't belong here."

The shifter's mouth quirked in a smile that didn't reach his eyes. "Your sanity is still in question. You allowed a bear to mate you, after all."

So, the stranger wasn't a bear. Another wolf, perhaps? A member of the rogue pack Everett had mentioned? Was he who Tomas had been arguing with earlier? Please Gods, let him have a conscience. It seemed he was some kind of mercenary, but even hired thugs had moral boundaries, right?

"Whose is the baby?" he demanded, his smile vanishing as quickly as it had come. "The bear's or the wolf's?"

"My mate's," I replied automatically, only realizing after I'd spoken that he shouldn't know I was pregnant. "How did you—"

"Some shifters are more sensitive to scent than others," he said, tapping the side of his nose. "Pregnant omegas have a subtly different scent."

I really hoped Tomas didn't possess the same keen sense of smell. He terrified me. At least this guy, whatever his agenda, didn't seem crazy. If Tomas believed me to be his mate and realized I was pregnant with another shifter's child, I was scared what he might do.

"Please get me out of here." I wasn't above begging if it kept me and my baby safe. "I literally met Tomas once. We went on one date, and it ended with me running away from him. I didn't even know shifters existed before then. Please believe me."

He groaned and dragged his hand down his face. "Fuck my life." He straightened. "Okay, here's what's going to happen. You'll stay here. You'll be strong. I'll see what I can do."

Fear seized my chest. It sounded like he was planning to leave me. "But why don't you just let me go?"

"Because," his tone was growing impatient, "I have a reputation to uphold. Who the hell would hire a backstabbing rat?"

He turned and headed toward the stairs. Dread pooled in my gut. Somehow, I knew that if he left, I'd never see him again, and I was afraid I wouldn't see the outside of this basement either.

"Please!"

He didn't stop.

CHAPTER

FORTY-THREE

E VERETT

"Hawk, report," Zander barked into a radio.

The radio crackled, then, "No sightings from the air above Moonlight Cove to the west of the river."

"Bea?" Zander said.

"None north of Main Street either," another voice replied.

"Everything looks normal, sir." This voice was Clay's. The officer was patrolling the streets of Moonlight Cove, looking for any sign of Milo. "The wolves are lying low. I haven't seen a single one since I arrived."

"Thanks. Keep searching." Zander returned the radio to his belt and raised his eyes to mine. "The Alpha has probably instructed his pack to stay indoors until this is over. It would be helpful if he picked up the damn phone when I call though."

After leaving the message with reception, nobody had been able to get back in touch with the rogue pack's Alpha.

"Excuse me, sir, you can't go in there!"

Zander and I spun around in time to see the receptionist chasing a tall, broad-shouldered alpha wolf in a leather

199

jacket. Before I'd consciously decided to act, I found myself across the room, pinning the wolf to the wall. His eyes flashed green, but they weren't contaminated by the piss yellow shade that indicated a wolf was turning feral, nor did this guy match the description of Tomas. Still, I was willing to bet he was involved somehow.

"Where is my mate?" I demanded, getting up in his face and letting my bear look out at him. My claws extended through the ends of my fingers and bit into his jacket.

The wolf cocked a brow. "You must be Milo's alpha."

"Where is he?" I repeated. "If you hurt one hair on his head, I'll rip your throat out."

To my surprise, the wolf didn't attempt to escape my grasp. Instead, he leaned close and inhaled. His eyes flashed green again.

"Start talking." Dad appeared at my side, authority emanating from him. His voice compelled the wolf to do as ordered. He dipped his head in submission, recognizing the clan's Alpha. Zander grabbed my shoulder and eased me away from them.

"What's going on?" Garrick asked from the doorway. "Suzy said you might need help."

"This wolf is about to tell us where we can find Milo," Dad said, his tone brooking no argument.

The wolf cleared his throat. "My name's Knox. I was hired to help retrieve a runaway omega with a mental disorder for his mate."

"You—" I started to lunge at him again, but Zander held me in place. "Milo is *my* mate."

Knox rolled his eyes. "Yeah, I figured that out on my own, thanks. The guy who hired me is a few sandwiches short of a picnic."

"So that's why you're here?" Zander asked. "You realized you unwittingly aided in an abduction?"

Knox shrugged. "Well, that, and I smelled my mate on Milo."

My hands twitched, desperate to curl around his throat. "Milo is *mine.*"

"Yes, I know. Back off, caveman. Milo isn't my mate, but he's been in contact with him. So have you. I scented him on you when you pinned me."

I shook my head, relieved not to have another alpha to fight. Whoever his mate was—presumably one of the ridge's locals—it wasn't important now.

"Do you know where Milo is?" Zander asked, echoing my earlier question.

"Yes." Knox nodded briskly. "He's in the basement of a house at 24 Linwood Lane in Moonlight Cove."

I opened my mouth, but he held up a hand to stop me.

"He's chained in place, but mostly unharmed."

"What do you mean by 'mostly'?" My tone was dangerously soft.

Nerves flickered through Knox's eyes. "Tomas knocked him over the head when we moved him into the house, and he looked like he might have been hit again, but he doesn't have any broken bones and his blood has pretty much stayed inside his body."

Pretty much. I wanted to smash things at the thought of Milo bleeding at all.

"Will you help us get him back?" Dad asked.

Knox grimaced. "I can't be seen helping you, but I'll tell you everything I can, and in return, I want to be introduced to my mate."

"Good. We can do that."

"But the mate comes after Milo is safely at home," I stressed.

"I understand."

Two painstaking hours later, under cover of the rapidly

descending darkness, two cars drove in convoy to the address in Moonlight Cove. I rode shotgun in Dad's vehicle, with Clay and Garrick in the back. Zander was driving the other, with more of his team and ours with him. We stopped a block away. I got out of the car, already shedding my clothes, and shifted. I paced restlessly along the roadside, waiting for the others to do the same. Just as Zander pulled up behind us, a scream pierced the air, and every hair on my body stood on end.

Milo.

FORTY-FOUR

MILO

I was cold down to my bones. The chill from the ground had zapped what little body heat I had, and I'd been trembling uncontrollably for what felt like hours. My teeth chattered, and my arms had long since gone numb. As I'd expected, I'd seen no sign of the other wolf after he'd left. Fortunately, I hadn't seen Tomas either. But now the door handle was turning, and I knew in my heart that my luck was about to change.

Tomas bounded down the stairs, his eyes still lit with that frightening yellow glow. He carried a pile of blankets. I wanted to snatch them off him and wrap myself in one, but I was completely at his mercy.

"You want these?" Tomas grinned as if he were pleased. "You can have them. All you need to do is be a good little mate."

I'm not your mate.

I didn't say it. I was smart enough not to aggravate him. He paused, no doubt waiting for me to ask what I'd have to do to get them. I didn't want to, but I also knew there was a good chance I'd get hypothermia if I didn't play along with his sick games, and I had a baby to protect. They had to be my number-one priority.

"What does that mean?" I asked reluctantly.

His grin widened. "We're going to fuck, and then I'm going to replace the mating bite from your false mate. Once the bond is complete, you can have the blankets. I might even bring you some stew."

I moistened my split lip. "That would be nice."

"Will you behave?"

I hesitated for a moment but then nodded. As it was, I was helpless, but if I played along and he freed me, I at least had a chance of defending myself or getting away from him.

"You won't bite or kick or hit me, or I'll do the same to you," Tomas warned.

"I won't," I lied. "I realize now that you're my true mate. I'm sorry for believing the stories my false mate told me."

Forgive me, Everett.

I'd lie, cheat, and steal if it meant getting out of here.

"Good."

Tomas put the blankets atop a stack of boxes and fished a key from his pocket. He approached me quickly, and I fought the urge to flinch. He unlocked my wrists and I bit my lip as sensation roared back into them, burning hot. I massaged the skin, hoping to lessen the sting, but it hurt like hell.

"Turn around and bend over," he said.

I did as he asked, my mind whirling at a million miles an hour. I could get out of this. It would be okay. If I just didn't think about what Tomas intended to do to me, I could hold out hope. He came around behind me and grabbed my hips. He bent over me and I heard him sniff. Then, before I could overthink it, I snapped by body up and smashed the back of my head into his face. He shouted in fury and released my hips. I sprinted for the door, my legs pumping as hard as they could, but before I reached the steps, he grabbed me and threw me to the floor.

I screamed, loud enough that I was sure any shifters in the neighborhood would have heard. Assuming we were in a neighborhood. We could be in the middle of the goddamn woods for all I knew.

"Fuck!"

He smacked me again. I bucked and fought, and when I caught his balls with my foot, he let go for long enough that I was able to lunge free again. At the top of the stairs, the door burst open and the most ruggedly handsome man I'd ever seen appeared. *Everett.* I threw myself into his arms and clung to him, soaking up the strength of his broad chest and steady heart. Other men rushed past him, but Everett cradled my head in his big hands, pressing my face into his shirt, so I couldn't see what was going on behind me.

"I knew you'd come," I whispered. "I knew you would."

For a guy who'd never been able to rely on anyone, that was pretty incredible.

"I'm here." Everett smoothed his hands down my back. "I've got you. You're safe, little mate."

I stretched onto my tiptoes and kissed him, then drew back and gazed at him as his eyes flicked from brown to gold and back again. It was obvious his bear wanted to come to the surface.

"You got him?" he called past me.

"Yeah." I recognized the voice as Zander's. "Clay, get the tranquilizer gun. There's no way Garrick and I can get him out of here without it."

I turned and saw that Everett's two older brothers had pinned Tomas to the ground. He was struggling, but he couldn't compete with the strength of two alpha bears. He slumped onto the dirt, but his yellow eyes never left me. A shiver tore through me, and Everett drew me into his arms.

"Let's get you out of here," he said.

I followed him up a couple of stairs, but then a clatter sounded below and one of the brothers shouted a warning. I glanced over my shoulder and froze in horror. Tomas had shifted. He lunged toward me, his teeth bared. I stumbled backward and fell on my ass. Pain exploded up my tailbone. Beside me, the air rippled. An instant later, Everett in his bear form intercepted Tomas. They crashed to the ground and rolled. Everett was on top, then Tomas, then Everett again. I started to cry out but pressed my hand to my mouth to silence myself. Everett couldn't afford to be distracted.

They growled, teeth clashed, and blood spattered the dirt. My stomach heaved. Luckily it was still empty. Everett came out on top, and before Tomas could reverse their positions again, Everett sank his teeth into the wolf's throat and tore out a chunk of flesh.

"Good Gods." I squeezed my eyes shut and retched again. When I opened my eyes, Everett stood in front of me, on his hind legs, blood soaking his front. Without thinking, I buried my face in his fur. His chest was heaving, but his breaths slowed while I held him. I couldn't get that image out of my mind. Everett had had to kill for me. He'd had to end another's life because of me. How the hell was I supposed to live with that?

Everett grunted, and his body rapidly shrank, his fur vanishing, until he stood naked and human in my arms. Without saying a word, he scooped me into his arms and carried me out.

FORTY-FIVE

EVERETT

I'd expected Milo to be disgusted by what I'd done in front of him. I'd killed someone, in a messy way, but even though I was naked and stained with Tomas's blood, he sat on my lap the entire drive home. Perhaps he was in shock.

"I'm sorry," I said softly. "You shouldn't have had to see that."

He looked up at me, his pale eyes shining with emotion. "And you shouldn't have had to do it. But you did, because of me."

"I would do anything to protect you." He needed to know that. If he was ever in danger again, this violent side of me, which I usually kept contained, would emerge to defend him. "I wish you hadn't seen me like that."

His eyes searched mine and then he dropped the lightest kiss on my lips. "You did nothing wrong, Ev." His voice was fierce with conviction. "Nothing."

I kissed him back, and cradled him against my chest. I hoped he'd keep that conviction once the shock had worn off.

Garrick cleared his throat. He was driving, since Zander, Dad, and the others had stayed behind to clean up and take care of any loose ends. "We're here."

I looked through the car window, surprised to see that we'd already stopped outside our house. The journey seemed to have taken no time at all. I opened the door and carried Milo out, ignoring his protests. He was featherlight and I wanted to keep him as close as possible.

"Thanks for the ride, brother."

"No problem." He tipped his head. "Take care of your mate. I'll drop by Momma's place to update her and Danny."

"I appreciate it."

My legs felt like lead as I climbed the doorstep. I used one hand to unlock the door while supporting Milo with the other.

"Can we shower?" he asked. "I'm so cold."

"You got it." I took him straight to the bathroom and turned on the shower. I dialed the heat down since getting into the water at its usual temperature would be too much for Milo's freezing body to handle. We'd have to warm him gradually.

He rested his head against my shoulder. "You'll join me, right?"

"If that's what you want." I worried that seeing the blood wash down the drain might be too much for him.

"I do."

I gently set him on his feet, then tested the water. It was lukewarm. A good starting point. I stepped under the spray, relieved to get rid of the metallic scent of Tomas's blood. Milo hovered just out of reach of the water until the worst of it was gone before joining me. He hissed as the water hit his skin.

"Is there anything I can do to help?" I hated to see him in pain.

He shook his head, his teeth gritted. Gradually, the tension eased from his jaw. He pressed his front against mine, looped his arms around me, and rested his cheek over my heart. I held him close, breathing in his familiar cherry scent. My heart ached. I'd come too close to losing him. If Tomas had hurt him, I'd never have forgiven myself. In a brief space of time, Milo had come to mean everything to me. Did he even know?

"I love you," I told him.

His arms tightened around me and he snuggled closer. "I love you, too."

He tilted his face up and I kissed him. Our mouths brushed, then separated. There was nothing sexual about it. The kiss was born of the need to connect with him and remind myself that he was here. I sensed the same was true for him. I reached behind him and turned the temperature up a notch.

"That's good." His skin was turning red and blotchy as color returned to it.

"So." I kissed his forehead. "You're pregnant?"

"Apparently." His tongue darted out and licked a drop of water from my chest. "I didn't even know that was possible."

"Neither did I," I admitted. "We haven't had any other human-shifter couples in Grizzly Ridge in my lifetime."

Milo pressed his lips together, looking uncertain. "Do you like kids?"

"I love kids." It was the truth. I'd love to have a brood of little bears to fuss over. "Are you... happy?"

The uncertainty dropped away and his mouth curved up. "I think I am. I want to give them all of the love, acceptance, and affection I didn't get when I was younger."

My heart clenched. "You will never go without those things again, for as long as I'm alive. I promise."

He softened against me. "I believe you." He gave a little sigh. "How did I get so lucky?"

I chuckled. "I'm the lucky one."

I'd literally torn someone's throat out in front of him, and he was still here. Not many people would be that loyal.

Milo shifted in my arms, drew back, and cranked the heat up higher. "Melinda said shifter pregnancies are different. What do you think mine will be like?"

"I don't know," I admitted. "We'll have to talk to the doctor, and maybe look up some reference books. Perhaps some of the more well-traveled or older clan members will know."

He nodded, but I could tell it unsettled him not to understand what was happening in his own body.

"We'll figure it out," I said.

He smiled and kissed me. "I know."

Once his body had returned to its normal temperature and we were both clean, we got out of the shower and dressed. When we emerged into the living room, most of my family was already there. Danny rushed over and pulled him into an embrace.

"I'm so glad you're okay!" he exclaimed. "We were scared for you. I'm sorry we weren't there to protect you. I should have gone into the restroom with you."

"It's okay," Milo said. "We couldn't have expected it. You guys found me, and that's the important thing." He made a thoughtful sound. "How did you find me?"

I met Dad's eyes. "We had a little help."

That was all we'd say about it for now, although I still had to uphold my end of our deal and help Knox find his mate later.

As soon as Danny released Milo, Momma gathered him

in a hug. Garrick gave him a bro-hug, and Dad rolled his eyes at Garrick's gesture and hugged him properly. Through the mate bond, I could sense Milo's emotions rolling through him. He felt warm. Secure. Welcome. He looked at me with big eyes, clearly beginning to realize that he had a family now. He took my hand and pressed against my side.

"They're your family too," I murmured, while my relatives pretended not to listen. "You're one of us."

He practically glowed. "You mean it?"

"One hundred percent."

FORTY-SIX

MILO

Everett and I sat side by side in a homey examination room at the local medical center. Doctor Black, a handsome older man with a silver mustache, was perched on a chair behind the desk.

"It's nice to meet you while you're conscious," he said with a little smile. "You do seem to have a knack for getting into trouble, don't you?"

My cheeks burned. "It's not my fault a crazy guy thought I was his mate."

His lips twitched. "Of course not." He cleared his throat. "So. You're pregnant."

"You don't need me to do another test to make sure?" I asked.

"That won't be necessary." He straightened and clasped his hands together on his lap. "My sense of smell is highly developed and can pick up on the subtle hormonal shifts omegas experience during pregnancy. I feel confident saying that you are, indeed, pregnant. Congratulations."

"Thanks." I beamed at Everett. I hadn't thought there was any doubt considering the test and what the wolf in the leather jacket had said about being able to smell the pregnancy, but there was something about having it confirmed by a medical professional that made it feel real.

"Is the baby healthy?" Everett asked.

"We'll need to do some tests to know for sure, but I see no reason to be worried. While I'm sure what happened yesterday was stressful, it shouldn't have been too physically traumatic. Add in the fact we're in the very early stages of pregnancy, and it's likely your cub will be just fine."

"So, it will be a cub?" I asked. "A shifter, not a human?"

His smile warmed. "I expect so. Shifter genes are dominant over most other species."

Okay, that was good to know. While the idea of raising a shifter child was terrifying because there was so little I knew about them, I also didn't want my baby to feel different from the other local children. I knew how it felt to know you didn't belong.

I pressed my lips together, wondering how to phrase my next question delicately. "Will the baby, erm, come out the same way as usual?"

Doctor Black's eyebrows shot up. "Do you mean, will you give birth to the baby anally?"

My cheeks flamed even hotter. "Um, yeah."

"Yes. Unless there are any complications, which we wouldn't expect from a pair of healthy males of good breeding age."

I squirmed in my chair. Good breeding age? Way to make us sound like livestock. Still, I had other questions I wanted to ask, so I scanned the list I'd written and found the next one.

"At what age will the baby be able to shift?"

Everett had already told me that most shifters could

shift from birth, although some had developmental delays, but our baby would be part human.

The doctor shrugged. "I would expect your cub to be the same as any other, despite having a human omega father. However, a delay of a few months wouldn't be anything to worry about."

"And the gestation period?" I asked.

"It's likely to be midway between the six months typical of a grizzly shifter and the nine months typical of a human. However, the progress of development will be greatly accelerated over the first month." His expression turned sympathetic. "You've already seen evidence of that with the morning sickness and the fact a test has given you a positive reading."

"So, I'll start showing more quickly?"

He seesawed his hand back and forth. "If it's one baby, you might have a small bump at the end of a month. If it's multiples, then yes."

"Wait. Multiples?" I glanced at Everett, who took my hand.

Doctor Black pulled a face, as though realizing he'd said something out of turn. "It's not uncommon for shifters to have multiples, unless they're on limiters. I don't suppose you are?"

"No. How many are we talking about here?" Because I wasn't sure I was mentally ready to deal with several children.

Everett squeezed my hand. "We'll find out as soon as we can. It's going to be fine, baby."

Gods, I hoped so.

FORTY-SEVEN

EVERETT

Later that night, Dad called a clan meeting. The clan gathered behind the Alpha's house, most in their human forms so they could nibble on the food Momma had prepared. I kept an eye on the assembled shifters, especially John and his friends, in case any of them expressed their bigoted attitude toward Milo. As far as I could tell, anyone who wasn't pleased by our mating was keeping their mouths firmly shut.

Dad's voice boomed through the yard as he summoned us. I wrapped my arm around Milo's shoulders and grabbed another bread roll for him as we passed the table. They were one of the few things he could eat without feeling nauseous, although Momma's home remedy was helping.

"Thank you all for coming," Dad said, his voice projecting effortless authority. "If you haven't already heard, Everett's mate Milo was abducted yesterday. Fortunately, we were able to locate him and bring him home before he came to any serious harm."

I glanced at Milo, my eyes narrowing at the sight of the bruise along his cheekbone. Fury scorched through me, and

I had to remind myself that Tomas had already paid for hurting him. I tucked him beneath my chin and held him close.

"That's not the only good news we have to share." He scanned the crowd, his chest puffed with pride. "Melinda and I are going to be blessed with our first grandchild. Milo is pregnant."

Applause nearly deafened me. Someone clapped my shoulder from behind, and Danny ruffled Milo's hair. Milo gazed up at me, his face lit with joy. I kissed him proudly, for all to see. We accepted congratulations, and then Dad gestured for quiet.

"We also have a new clan member. I'd like to introduce Knox Kingston."

Knox stepped onto the deck beside Dad and raised his chin. Irritation prickled through me. I appreciated that Knox had helped me get Milo back, but he'd been behind the wheel when Tomas had kidnapped Milo, so I didn't trust the guy. At least, not fully. He'd only come to us because he'd seen a way to get something he wanted: access to his mate.

As Knox's gaze swept the shifters, his eyes switched from brown to green and his fangs dropped. His nostrils flared and he took a step forward. I looked around, frowning. On the other side of Milo, Danny's eyes had turned golden and his teeth showed between his lips, but far from looking pleased, as Knox did, his eyes were wide and terrified. He spun on his heel, tore off his clothes, and shifted. Others sprang out of the way as he bolted into the woods. I lurched after him, ready to follow, but Milo grabbed my sleeve.

"Let him go," he said. "He needs space."

I hesitated, reluctant to leave Danny alone when he was clearly upset, but I knew that as an omega Milo was in a better position to understand what he needed than me, so after a moment I nodded and wrapped my mate in my arms again.

Dad whistled to get everyone's attention. "Knox is a wolf shifter, and he'll be staying with Melinda and me until he finds a rental. If anyone knows of a house he might be interested in, let us know. That's all for now. Enjoy your run."

Shifters began stripping off their clothes, but I didn't follow their lead. No way was I leaving Milo alone when I knew some of the clan might not be thrilled by our news—not even to follow Danny. A pair of teachers from the school stopped by to congratulate us, as did Skye from the bakery. I kissed Milo's head, feeling his relief through our bond. But then he stiffened. I glanced up and spotted what he already had—John and one of his buddies were coming toward us.

"Want me to get you out of here?" I whispered in his ear.

"No." He straightened and squared his shoulders. "It's all right."

Pride surged through me. That was my brave omega.

"John," I said as they drew near. I nodded to his companion. "Trav."

"Evening, Everett." John lowered his gaze to Milo. "Hello, Milo."

"Hi, John."

Tension filled the air between us. It felt like a standoff where no one knew what to say next.

"I'm sorry about what happened to you." John's face was rapidly turning the color of tomato and his tone was gruff, but he held Milo's gaze. "Congratulations on the pregnancy. Doc Black told us the cub will be a shifter. Perhaps you're one of us after all."

Milo didn't reply for a long moment—probably as

shocked by John's words as I was. "Thank you," he said simply. "That means a lot."

John grunted, and he and Trav moved past us, yanking their jackets off. Milo turned in my arms.

"Well, that was unexpected," he said.

I laughed. "Tell me about it." I racked my mind, wondering what had brought about the sudden change. "Maybe the fact you can give birth to shifter children outweighs the fact you're not a shifter."

"Maybe." He shrugged. "I don't really care. It was good of him to try to make peace, but I don't think we're going to be friends anytime soon."

"Fair enough." I kissed him, so he'd know I didn't care what he decided about which members of the clan he wanted to socialize with. He gasped and pressed closer, grinding his half-hard cock against my leg. I started to harden in response. Milo whimpered against my mouth.

"Hey."

I growled at Knox, who'd dared to interrupt. "What?"

He tugged on the end of his ponytail. "My mate... did he just reject me?"

Sighing, I let Milo go. "I wouldn't say that."

"Then what was it?" He looked lost. "I thought when I met my mate, they'd want me as much as I wanted them."

I pulled a face. Ugh. I did not want to discuss my brother's love life, nor did I want to share details of his romantic history behind his back. "The bear who ran away, you're sure he's your mate?"

His eyes narrowed and flashed green. "Yes. Why?"

"He's my little brother."

"Oh." He looked surprised. "He's much hotter than you."

I grumbled, but Milo snuggled against my side, so I let

the comment go. I didn't care what Knox thought of me. I had all the mate I needed.

"Danny, my brother, was in a bad relationship recently. I won't tell you more than that. You'll have to ask him yourself. But the point is, he's wary of getting hurt again, so you'll have to be patient with him."

Knox's thundercloud of an expression made me feel better about this development. It was obvious he didn't like the thought of Danny in pain. "I'll be as patient as it takes."

"Good, because if you mess with him, I'll tear you apart."

He smirked. "Understood."

We shook on it. I hid a smile. He had no idea how much work lay ahead if he wanted to win Danny's battered heart.

FORTY-EIGHT

MILO

The morning after the clan run, Everett returned to work and I helped Melinda make bread rolls and vegetable soup for the children's home. For some reason, the smell of vegetables cooking didn't turn my stomach the way meat did—to the horror of every bear shifter in my new family—so we'd be eating more vegetables, at least until my morning sickness abated.

When we arrived at the home, our arms laden with food, the door opened as we approached. To my surprise, it was Sam, not one of the younger kids, who raced down the stairs.

"Thank Gods you're okay!" Sam called. They stopped short, panting slightly. "I was so scared when I heard you were taken. Did they hurt you?"

My heart warmed at Sam's concern. In my old life, I could have vanished for a week, and I'm not sure anyone would have noticed. Here, people cared, and I couldn't overstate how much that meant.

"Nothing I couldn't handle," I said.

"And you're pregnant?"

I smiled. "I am."

We made our way to the door and Sam held it open, following on my heels to the kitchen. Melinda trailed behind. As soon as I put the containers of bread rolls on the counter, Sam hugged me. Their embrace was strong considering how slender they were.

"Please tell me they didn't scare you away," Sam said, drawing back. "Are you staying in Grizzly Ridge?"

My smile drew. "I am."

"Yay!" They hugged me again, then let me go.

A throat cleared behind us. I turned to see George wearing a concerned expression and tugging at his pink bow tie.

"You're unharmed?"

"Yes." At this point, I wondered if I should call everyone into the kitchen to make a group announcement.

"Fabulous." He tilted his head toward the hall. "There's something I'd like to ask you. Will you talk to me in my office?"

I raised an eyebrow at Melinda, who stood beside him, but she just shrugged. Apparently, she didn't know what he wanted either. "Sure."

George led me into to his office. He sat behind his desk, which was stacked high with papers and books, and I took the only other chair.

"I hear you're moving to the ridge," he said, propping his elbows on the desk and steepling his fingers.

"That's right." I wondered where this was going.

"Do you have a job lined up?"

"Not yet." I didn't have particularly high hopes, either. There were no accountancy firms in Grizzly Ridge. Or at least, not any that I'd seen.

"Hmm." George leaned toward me, his eyes sparkling. "Our accounts aren't in great shape."

My heart sped up. "I'm sorry to hear that."

"We would also like to bring in more donations so we can improve our facilities."

I nodded. Their facilities were much better than what I'd grown up with, but there was always room for improvement.

He looked up at the ceiling, as if asking for patience, then his eyes flicked back to me. "Would you consider coming on as our financial manager? You have the skills to improve our accounts, and I'm sure you could figure out how to attract more donors."

My heart was racing now. "Are you offering me a job?"

"Yes, Milo." He flashed me a smile. "The children like you, and you understand how it feels to be in their shoes. I can't think of anyone better for the role."

Yes. I wanted to scream it from the ceiling. I'd anticipated it being difficult to find work, but here George was, offering me a job that I was not only qualified for, but that I'd actually care about. Unfortunately, there was a topic we needed to address before I could agree to anything.

"Have you heard that I'm pregnant?"

"Yes." His expression softened. "Congratulations."

"Thank you." I hesitated, then continued, "After they're born, it might be difficult for me to work, at least for the first few years."

"You can have paternity leave immediately after the birth, and we'll be flexible. The hours won't be full time, and as long as the work gets done, I don't care when you do it or where from. Although the children might like to see you from time to time."

"That sounds too good to be true."

He winked. "Then say yes, and we'll work the rest out later."

"Yes," I said. "I would love to work for you."

"Perfect." He straightened and tidied a stack of paper. "Welcome aboard."

George and I rejoined the others, and Melinda and I stayed for lunch. As soon as we got home again, I excused myself to call Everett.

"I got a job!" I said when he answered.

"Congratulations, baby." His warm tone rumbled through me. "That was fast."

"I know, right? George asked me to work with him at the children's home." I explained what he wanted me to do and how flexible he was willing to be.

"That sounds perfect for you," he said when I finished talking. "You're going to be great."

"Do you think so?" Nerves flopped around in my stomach. "I hope so. I want to do my best for those kids."

"You will." He cleared his throat. "I have to go, but I'll see you later, baby. I love you."

"I love you too."

After the call ended, I clutched the phone to my chest and grinned at nothing. I'd never felt so full of joy and hope in my life.

FORTY-NINE

EVERETT

I ushered Danny out of the house and closed the front door with a sigh of relief. I loved my family, and I was grateful they were going out of their way to make Milo feel welcome, but I wanted my mate to myself. New mates were expected to lock themselves inside for days without being seen, but because of the circumstances surrounding Milo's arrival in town, we hadn't had that. Well, it started now.

"They're gone?" Milo asked after returning from the bathroom, where he'd vanished after Garrick had thoughtlessly mentioned the rubbery eggs he'd had for lunch. Even the word "eggs" seemed to set Milo off. Fortunately, Momma was experienced with pregnant omegas and had been able to help prepare a dinner that wouldn't make him ill.

"It's just you and me, baby." I tugged him tenderly into my embrace, being careful not to hold him too tightly in case it upset his already unsettled stomach. "Let's snuggle."

He smiled wearily up at me. "My favorite."

I kissed his forehead and guided him to the bed. I

flopped on top, stretched along the length of the mattress, and he positioned himself beside me and cuddled up to my side.

"Feeling better?" I asked.

"A little." He rested his head over my heart and the organ seemed to swell and throb, trying to get closer to him.

"Good." I smoothed my hand over his hair. "I've taken the rest of the week off work so we can have time to ourselves."

His mouth curved in the most beautiful smile I'd ever seen. "That sounds perfect."

"I'm going to miss you next week."

Milo's boss had asked him to come in for his last week to make sure everything was ready for the handover to a new accountant.

"Are you sure you'll be okay by yourself?" I asked.

"Ev." His tone was stern. "Tomas is dead. I'm safe. It will be fine."

I huffed. I'd rather go with him, and I had the leave, but he insisted on doing it by himself. I knew I needed to make an effort not to smother him with overprotectiveness, so I'd agreed. Reluctantly.

Perhaps a topic change was in order. "Are you excited to start your new job after that?"

"I am." He yawned, and covered his mouth. "At my current job, I just move money around. Working with George, I feel like I'll actually be able to make a difference." His cheeks colored and he searched my eyes, as if trying to see what I thought of that.

"The kids will be lucky to have you." I curled my arm around his waist. "I'm glad you were able to find a good job so quickly." I'd felt guilty for asking him to move away from everything he knew and had fought for, so it was a relief to know he had a job he was excited about.

"It's like it was meant to be."

I smiled to myself. More like it was *fated*.

"You know, I never doubted you." Milo's tone was growing sleepy. "Tomas tried to convince me that I didn't matter to you, and that we weren't true mates, but I knew you'd come, and that all I had to do was stay safe until then." He drew in a slow breath. "It's the first time in my life I truly believed I mattered to someone."

Emotion clogged my throat. I nuzzled the top of his head.

"I'll always be there for you," I promised. "Always."

He sniffed. I glanced down. Were those tears glimmering in his eyes? My chest tightened.

"Don't cry, baby," I pleaded. "We're here now. We're safe."

His lips trembled. "They're happy tears. I always wanted to be someone's first choice, and to know they'd do anything for me, and now I have that. You've got no idea how much it means to me."

"Sweet Milo." I tilted his face up and brushed his lips with mine. "You're not just my first choice. You're my only choice. There will never be anything or anyone who comes before you. I swear it."

"I love you, Everett. My alpha."

I buried my face in his hair and breathed in his cherries and vanilla scent. "I love you too, my omega."

FIFTY

MILO

Christmas day began with carols and brunch at Melinda and Aaron's house. My heart was light as we laughed over our meal, and I caught Everett watching me affectionately several times. He knew how much it meant to me to be able to share Christmas with a family. I'd never had a festive season like this, with merriment and gifts exchanged. Most years in whatever home I was in, I might have gotten an extra hot chocolate and perhaps a candy cane, but Melinda had gone all out— and I'd helped as much as she'd let me. I suspected she'd gone overboard because of me, and the thought brought tears to my eyes as I smiled across the table at her. I'd been crying at the drop of a hat lately, but at least the morning sickness had ended.

After brunch, we gathered around the tree to exchange gifts. I practically bounced in my seat, excited to see what my family thought of the gifts I'd bought for them. For Melinda, I had a new pie pan, since hers had seen better days. When she opened it, she beamed and gathered me into one of those maternal hugs I loved so much. For Aaron,

I'd bought a bottle of his favorite honey-infused whiskey. For Garrick, a new lure for fishing in the stream—which he liked to do in his human form as well as his bear form. He shot me a grin, and I felt a flash of joy that I'd gotten it right. I'd listened every time he'd talked about his supplies, so I knew what he had and what he didn't.

I'd given Zander a new hat—the same brand as the one that rarely left his head. He put it on immediately and tossed me the old one. I donned it at a jaunty angle, my heart so full it felt like it might burst. I passed Danny his prettily wrapped present and waited while he tore into it and exclaimed with delight at the cute, patterned cupcake cases. Finally, I handed Everett the last of my gifts, gnawing my lip. Would he like it?

He peeled the tape off carefully, his big fingers more graceful than they had any right to be, and he set the delicate paper to the side. He chuckled and raised his eyes to mine.

"Exactly what I need." He held the necklace up for his family to see. A gold bear hung from a fine chain, with two words engraved into the metal. *Papa Bear.* He threaded it around his neck and fastened it on, then leaned over and kissed me. "Thank you, baby."

"I hope you like it," I whispered.

"Of course I do. It represents our new family."

I threw my arms around him, thrilled that he'd been able to tell what I was trying to communicate. "It does."

"Too cute," Danny protested. "Some of us are still single, you know?"

Everett and I exchanged a look. We both knew that Danny could be mated in seconds if he wanted to, but he was keeping Knox at a distance. Considering Danny's past and how intimidating Knox was, I understood it, but I was amazed he was able to stand his ground. I'd been drawn to

Everett very strongly, and I was sure he experienced something similar.

"Here." Everett handed me a box. "This is from me."

The box wasn't wrapped. Just simple black velvet. I flipped it open and gawked at the large diamond ring nestled inside. My gaze flew to Everett's.

He gazed at me in a way I'd dreamed of seeing for my whole life. "According to shifter tradition, we're as good as married now, but I want everyone—including humans—to know you're mine. Marry me?"

"Yes." I plucked the ring out and slid it onto my finger. It fit perfectly. "How did you—?"

He winked. "I know all your measurements, baby."

Danny groaned. "Please stop."

"Never." Everett's lips found mine, and this kiss wasn't brief.

We only parted when Garrick wolf-whistled. "Get a room," he complained.

I grinned at Everett. "Soon?"

"The second we're done here," he agreed.

Melinda laughed when Everett's brothers started another round of protests. "It'll be your turn before long," she warned them.

That shut them up.

EPILOGUE

E VERETT
I strolled through the house after arriving home from work and looked for Milo. He hadn't been on the sofa, where he should be resting. His due date was only a few days away, and he was supposed to be taking it easy. I checked the kitchen, but it was empty. I found him in the master bedroom, and stopped to stare in awe. He'd clearly been hard at work. The windows were covered with fabric, a pair of lamps I'd never seen before stood on each side of the bed, and the thermostat had been turned up until it was warm and stuffy.

Milo glanced up at me, a dazed look in his eyes, then turned back to the mountain of cushions and fluffy blankets he'd piled on the bed. No, not just piled. Arranged. Artfully.

"It's not right," he said. "I need a purple throw, but we don't have one. The den won't be perfect without it."

I narrowed my eyes. "Den?"

"For our baby." A scan had revealed we were only having one, but we'd opted not to learn their gender. "It needs a cozy den to come home to."

The back of my neck prickled. Milo was nesting. Pregnant omega shifters often nested soon before giving birth, but I hadn't expected it of him since he was human. The shifter baby inside of him must be influencing his behavior.

"Come and sit down," I urged. "I'll call Momma to see if she has a purple throw." And because I suspected the baby would be here soon.

"But—"

"It's a beautiful den," I told him, and he preened. "You did well, omega. Now you need to rest so our baby knows it's time to come into the world."

"I did well?" The glaze cleared from his eyes and he smiled.

I pulled him as close as his belly would allow and kissed him. "Yes, it's perfect, and so are you."

He looked down, a blush rising on his cheeks. He let me steer him to the living room, but winced as he tried to sit.

"Are you okay?" I asked.

He grimaced. "Just a twinge in my lower back."

Alarm bells jangled in my mind. "Is it the first time that's happened?"

"No, I've been feeling them for an hour or so."

Definitely time to call Momma and the doctor.

"Wait here." I called Momma, then Doctor Black, and once they'd both assured me they were on their way, I filled a hot water bottle and took it to Milo. "For your back."

He took it gratefully. "Thanks."

I sat beside him and took his hand. He positioned the water bottle behind himself and rested his head on my shoulder, but after only a couple of seconds, he shot upright again, his eyes wide.

"I think I peed myself," he whispered. He stood slowly. The back of his sweatpants were soaked.

"You didn't pee yourself," I said. "The baby is on its way."

"Oh." His shoulders slumped with relief. "Thank Gods. That's less humiliating."

At that moment, there was a knock on the door. I put my arm around Milo's shoulders and ushered him out, pausing to grab our birthing bag from beside the door. I opened it and thrust the bag at Momma.

"His water broke," I said. "We need to go."

She nodded. "I'll sort him out. You get the car."

A shudder racked Milo's body and he whimpered. I glanced at Momma, not sure how I was supposed to leave him when he was clearly in pain.

"Go," she ordered.

Reluctantly, I got the car from the garage and drove it around the front of the house. Milo and Momma got in the back seat. I waited until the doors had shut and then pulled away, careful to avoid jostling Milo as much as possible. On the way, I called Doctor Black and asked to meet him at the clinic instead.

When we arrived, he was already waiting in front with a wheelchair. I helped Milo into the chair and wheeled it behind Doctor Black to the delivery room. I lifted Milo onto the bed and while Momma and the doctor fussed over him, I sent a quick message to our family chat, letting them know that Milo was going into labor.

I claimed the chair beside the bed and clasped Milo's hand.

"How are you doing?" I asked.

He gave me a shaky smile. "So far, so good."

Unfortunately, it didn't stay that way for long. Once the baby decided they were coming, they were determined to enter the world as soon as possible. The contractions ramped up quickly. Milo's face was pale, his forehead beaded with sweat.

"You've got this, baby," I told him, hardly able to believe how strong he was. People said omegas were the weaker secondary gender, but I would never make the mistake of believing that after seeing Milo strain to bring our child into the world, one contraction at a time.

"They're crowning," Doctor Black said. "We need a big push, Milo. Three, two—"

Milo's face scrunched with effort. His breathing caught. I'm pretty sure one of my fingers snapped in his grip. And then, after what felt like an eternity, we heard a small gurgle. Milo closed his eyes, a smile of relief spreading across his face, and a moment later, the gurgle became a cry. The nurse took the baby from Doctor Black and wiped them clean, then bundled them in a blanket.

"Would you like to see her?" she asked.

"Her?" I croaked.

The nurse beamed. "Congratulations, Daddy. You have a baby girl."

She passed our baby to me and I scooted closer to Milo. Momma stood behind my shoulder.

"Look, Milo," I said. "Our little girl."

His eyelids lifted wearily and he gazed down at her, his expression awash with all the love currently expanding in my own chest. "She's beautiful." He ignored the nurse, who'd started cleaning him up, and kissed our baby's forehead. "Kimberly."

My eyes prickled, and my heart felt so full it could burst. The two of them together were the most wonderful thing I'd ever seen, and I knew I'd be happy every day that I got to spend with them. "She's going to be the most loved baby in Grizzly Ridge."

"We'll make sure of it," Momma agreed. "By the way,

the rest of the family is outside. Are you feeling up to seeing them, Milo?"

Milo's smile lit him from the inside out. "I would love to see our family."

I loved the way he said "our." My family had welcomed him into the fold, and he was as much a part of it as me. Now, Kimberly would be blessed with three overprotective uncles and the most adoring grandparents she could dream of. I kissed the top of her head, and then Milo's.

"I love you both so much."

THE END

ABOUT THE AUTHOR

A.J. Cane writes LGBTQIA+ paranormal romance with love interests who will make you swoon. A.J. can usually be found reading, writing, or eating way too much chocolate.

www.ingramcontent.com/pod-product-compliance
Lightning Source LLC
Chambersburg PA
CBHW032252310726
48973CB00008B/2392